A Shining Path

L.S. JOHNSON

Traversing Z Press
San Leandro, California
www.traversingz.com

ISBN (paperback): 979-8-9857972-1-3
ISBN (ebook): 979-8-9857972-0-6
Library of Congress Control Number: 2022903096

The following works are quoted in this book:
"There is a land of pure delight," written by Isaac Watts, ca. 1709
"Soldiers of Christ, arise," written by Charles Wesley, ca. 1749
The Tempest, written by William Shakespeare, ca. 1610–1611

TABLE OF CONTENTS

He maketh a path to shine after him;
one would think the deep to be hoary.
Upon earth there is not his like, who is made without fear.
He beholdeth all high things: he is a king over
all the children of pride.
—Job 41:32–34

PART I

The Journey

CHAPTER I

Decisions and Promises

It is a strange thing to be orphaned. For the first time in my life I was without familial ties to either support or constrain me. My father was gone, my home about to pass to my distant cousin; there was nothing left of the Caroline I had once been. I was, of course, tied to Jo—or *partnered*, as we both preferred, for our companionship was by choice. But she was as adrift as I, having been cast out of her own family. Grief-stricken, unmoored, we might have given ourselves up for lost, but we both craved *purpose*—and there was the more mundane concern of our finances. Jo's family had confiscated her accounts, and while I still had my own funds, without some further income my monies could only provide for our longer-term subsistence. Thus, we fell back on the one trade that could employ us both: we once again became agents for hire and agreed to help Mr. Smith find Mrs. Masterson, ending the threat of the Leviathan once and for all.

Once we had decided, we moved swiftly. I kept to the letter of the entailment, which obligated me to leave my cousin the house, land, and furniture—and not a candle more. All the household goods, all the books and paintings and keepsakes, all the clothes and tools and even the boot scraper at the door were either given to the Simmonses or crated for storage. I would have preferred to supervise the removal, but already missives were arriving daily from Mr. Smith: the players in this last act were taking their places, plots were in motion. There was no time; there was never any time, not in this business—

But on how these machinations had cost me those last days with my father, I did not dwell. I knew his end had been swift, and he had wanted me to help protect England. It was enough. It had to be enough.

We delegated the final removal to the Simmonses, their last job for us. They had worked for my father since before I was born, and Mrs. Simmons had raised me after my mother passed. Bidding them farewell felt another blow, though softened by promises of future visits. That Mrs. Simmons embraced Jo, man's suit and all, warmed my heart. After so much unease on the former's part it seemed a kinship had blossomed, and Jo was so moved by the gesture that she had to walk away for a moment to master herself. The sight of their two pale figures waving goodbye from the doorway of my childhood home was a bittersweet feeling the likes of which I had never experienced before. That intensity of emotion stayed with me until we finally boarded the ship for Dormouth. As we drew away from the low, foggy coastline, so dear to my heart, I found myself suddenly weeping. Jo held me and I cried into the soft grey wool of her coat, watching over her shoulder as the coast vanished into fog.

"Darling," Jo whispered. "Is it your father, or the house, or—?"

"Everything," I managed, my voice shuddering. In that moment she felt my only anchor in the world.

"We don't have to do this," Jo said. When I started to speak again, she hushed me. "No, hear me out, Caro. No one would blame you for wanting to take time to grieve. Smith has others he can turn to. He can rally troops if need be."

"We've had this argument already," I gasped. "Rally them to what cause? To fight a creature so monstrous it defies description, controlled through a kind of sorcery? What minister, what general would believe such a thing?"

Jo drew out her handkerchief and dabbed at my eyes for me. "Be that as it may, it does not have to be *us*. It does not have to be *you*."

I fell silent, letting her wipe my face like I was a child as I untangled my thoughts. Finally, I said, "But no one cares as we do. Even when it was just poor Emily missing, no one cared as we do. There is so much wrong in the world," I continued. "So much evil, so much cruelty. But this one thing *we* can make right." My voice dropped to a whisper. "My father would have wanted me to try, I'm certain of it."

She kissed me then and held me. "Then we will make it right," she whispered into my hair. "For Theophilus."

"For Theophilus," I agreed.

It was not until we were in our tiny cabin for the night that I trusted myself to say the one thing that had been pressing on me since our decision. "Jo," I whispered.

"What, darling?" she asked, curling around me, her brown hair soft against my skin. What a strange world, that brought me such joy at the price of so much death. What would it be like, to be like any other couple: a cottage somewhere, steady work, church on Sundays? To have never watched a monster eat a man, or felt a man's lifeblood running over my hands?

"I want you to promise me one thing," I whispered.

She was silent, but her arm tightened around my waist.

"No matter what, we do not separate. None of this 'you to do one thing and I another.' I cannot, I *will not* lose you too. Whatever we face, we face it together. If this is our fated end, we end together. Promise me, Jo. Please."

Jo propped herself up on one elbow, studying my face. "Caro," she said quietly, "you know as well as I how chaotic matters can become, all in an eyeblink. A promise like that could hamstring us."

But I was shaking my head. Again, I was overcome by emotion. Was it grief, or fear? I could not say, but it overwhelmed me. In that moment, her promise seemed the most important thing in the world.

She must have sensed my anguish, because she caught my gaze and held it, her grey eyes nearly black in the shadows. "Here is what I will promise," she continued. "I promise that we will *decide* together, and we will *act* together. I cannot promise more than that, Caro. I will not sacrifice us both for fear of a momentary parting." Her voice dropped to a whisper. "I know I have failed you on this before. I will not fail you this time. I swear to you: no separation unless our very lives depend on it."

I took a breath. "*Our* lives," I said. "Not *my* life. Because I do not have one without you."

Again, she met my gaze squarely. "Our lives," she agreed. In the small, stuffy cabin, the water lapping beneath us, the words seemed to have a weight of their own. Our lives, together. As we had begun that night in Harkworth Hall, as we had been since. Her lips found mine, sealing her vow; I slid my fingers into the thick waves of her hair and parted my legs to her.

CHAPTER II

Dormouth

*O*ur boat followed the coast of England southwards, an uneasy echo of my journey to London. Then my father was alive, and I could only think of Jo, not yet knowing the trials she faced with her family. Now we both stood upon the deck and watched as the land gave way to the mouth of the Thames. Once our navy had fought the Leviathan to a standstill here; of that battle there was no sign, and I struggled now to imagine such horror amidst the sun-dappled water.

We passed the white cliffs of Dover, as remarkable as poetry and song had expressed, but we were bound for a different port. Penelope Brocas, who had murdered several men at the behest of Mrs. Masterson, whose paintings were doorways to a place called Arcadia, who had viciously attacked Mr. Morrow and myself—oh! Mr. Smith was playing a cunning game with her. First, he had contrived to let her escape, then had her followed, in hopes she would lead us to Mrs. Masterson and the Leviathan. Our last letter from him reported that Miss Brocas had booked a coach to Dormouth. From this southern port a ship could be had for almost any destination in the world. The Masterson plot, it seemed, might no longer restrict itself to mere upheaval between England and France.

At last we arrived, tired and a little queasy from a spell of rough water, both of us pinked from sun and wind. Rocky beaches gave way to the town's edges as we steered our way to the sheltering bay. The beaches were not unlike those in Arcadia, where I had last seen the Leviathan—and its clutch of offspring. There had been so many eggs—if even one of them hatched, and we faced not one but two Leviathans, or God help us, *several*—

Jo leaned close to me, her hat shadowing us both. "We still have choices," she murmured in my ear. "We will hear him out, but we can also leave. Not—" she quelled my reply with a squeeze of my arm— "not that I am suggesting we abandon our duty. But I won't undertake foolish risks."

I looked at her, marveling at how easily she divined my unease. "*We* won't undertake foolish risks," I amended, and was rewarded with a ridiculous kiss on the tip of my nose.

We descended the gangplank, Jo helping me over the last step. For a moment, all was noise and confusion amidst the bustling pier—and then we sighted the brown-suited figure of Mr. Windham, waving vigorously beside a plain coach. The sight of his familiar, ruddy face, so beloved of my father, brought on a wave of renewed grief. Still, I managed to smile as we drew near.

"Miss Daniels," he began as soon as we were close, his eyes gleaming with emotion. "Thank you for coming so soon after … that is, we all felt your loss—"

I silenced him by clasping his hands. We gazed at each other, my own eyes welling, and then he smiled sadly. "Well. I bid you welcome, though would that the circumstances were more pleasant. Chase," he continued, shaking Jo's hand. "We're in both your debts for this one. It is a murky business, and the foreign aspect makes it most delicate. We have had a devil of a time finding men who fully understand the need for secrecy, and Morrow is still not completely recovered."

"Surely he's not working on this!" I exclaimed. After his vicious stabbing by Miss Brocas, Mr. Morrow had been ordered to several weeks of rest and recovery. I had thought his sister would be enough to ensure his obedience, but perhaps even her willfulness had been overcome.

"He keeps offering his services and we keep refusing, but I know what happens when active men are confined too long." Mr. Windham helped me in the coach, then stepped aside so Jo could settle beside me. "I would not be surprised if he turns up."

"If he waits too long there may be nothing to turn up for," Jo remarked, moving her legs aside so Mr. Windham could get in. As he struck the roof of the coach, she continued, "Has Miss Brocas booked passage?"

"Not just passage for herself—a whole ship." He leaned forward as the coach began a slow, clacking transit. "She sails in two days, maybe three. She's staying at the southern end of town. We're at an inn further down the coast so we don't accidentally cross paths with her. Her cargo is being loaded now, and most of the passengers seem to have arrived."

"Passengers?" Jo frowned at him. "What passengers?"

"The so-called Arcadians." Mr. Windham mimicked her expression. "Didn't Smith explain? Well. He has had much to see to ... he told you of her activities in London, yes?"

"He told us of her escape, and her subsequent purchases," I clarified. After her escape, Miss Brocas had returned to London and taken lodgings in Seven Dials, venturing out in disguise to buy large quantities of pigments, oils, and canvas before making arrangements for her journey south.

"Well, shopping wasn't all she did. She spent her evenings at various meetings in London. Political meetings," he explained at our confused looks. "The abolition of slavery. Challenges to enclosure laws. Labor and penal reforms. At each one she handed out cards." He drew out his pocketbook, from which he produced a small, rectangular paper. "We managed to acquire a few."

A New Life in Arcadia
Hope   Prosperity   Tolerance
A new country founded on the principles of
TRUTH and PEACE
All Are Welcome

"But Arcadia isn't *real*," Jo said.

"And yet we both stood upon its ground," I put in. Did she think we had imagined it? "We breathed its air. Plants grew there, birds flew through its skies."

"But it's not *here*, not the way Dormouth is, or London … It cannot be, or else why this palaver with the paintings? It's more like a, a *conjuration*. Not a place on a map, with laws and, and currency, and houses …"

"But perhaps that is the appeal," I said. I was without a home now. If I were persecuted in some fashion as well? I might risk all in a new land, even one accessible only through magic.

"I think Miss Daniels is closer to it, but not quite," Mr. Windham said. "Wherever the paintings may lead, this Arcadia is indeed a real place. That ship is bound for an island somewhere in the Channel, yet apparently outside the remit of both England and France. Mr. Smith is working with a French counterpart to try and determine where exactly this island is, and if either of our countries can lay claim to it, but so far we have come up with nothing. Every spit of land between us has long been accounted for."

"Unless Missus Masterson is thinking to sink the ship as food for the creature, as her son did?" Jo asked.

"But that would mean Miss Brocas would be lost to her." He shook his head. "No, I think somehow Arcadia is real, and many are willing to try a new start there. A place without the persecutions or hindrances of England, far closer than the colonies? I can see where many would be tempted."

"Save for the resident monster, I might also be tempted," Jo said. "Where, dare I ask, is Missus Masterson in this?"

"Our ultimate quarry has not been seen." He angled his head at the coast. "We suspect she is waiting on Arcadia— wherever Arcadia lies."

At this pronouncement we fell silent. That there might be many innocents, lured by false promises to Mrs. Masterson's side, was a complication I had not considered. Did she intend to give them this promised haven? Or did she intend to use them in some fouler manner? Her sons had happily thrown many unfortunate souls into the beast's maw. To keep several such creatures sated—

Where will you be, when I remake the foundations of the world?

But I did not want to think on Mrs. Masterson's grandiose pronouncements, or her monsters; we would face those horrors soon enough. Instead, I turned my gaze to the coastline. It was like the northern coast that I knew so well, and yet not. Everything seemed a little softer, a little brighter, as if it had been painted by a gentler hand. The road rose and dipped, twisted and turned, wending its way through scrubby grasses and stunted trees, until finally we came to a village facing another, smaller bay. The snugness of the houses, the way the villagers hailed each other from long acquaintanceship, it all made my heart ache. Would I ever again be part of such community? *Orphan*, it seemed, could have several meanings.

We rounded a last bend and halted before an inn, a timbered building gleaming with whitewash. Mr. Windham helped me down, directing us to go straight to the back while he saw to our baggage. Inside was warm and cozy. We glimpsed a little dining room with a fire banked low, and a narrow taproom with its requisite locals huddled over pints and talking animatedly. If nothing else, it seemed we would be able to spend a night or two in comfort.

"Straight to the back" led us to a private dining room whose table was covered in papers. At the head of the table sat Mr. Smith, his bewigged, brown head bowed over a letter, in all likelihood a report from one of his many spies. When he heard the door open, he looked up sharply, squinting behind his pince-nez, then a smile broke over his face and he rose to greet us.

"Miss Daniels," he said warmly, bowing as he clasped my hand. "And Chase. May I say how sorry I was to hear of your father's passing."

I merely inclined my head. While Mr. Windham, I knew, had spoken from the heart, I was not so certain about Mr. Smith's sentiments. That he felt affection for all he employed, and especially Jo, I believed; but I also knew that his true loyalty was to England, and there was little he would stop at to protect his king and country—and he could rouse those same instincts in Jo.

"What news of Miss Brocas?" Jo asked as she settled me in a chair and sat beside me.

"Straight to the point as always." Mr. Smith flashed Jo a brief smile as he closed the door and sat back down with a flick of his coattails. "Let us see now. We have a team of men watching Missus Loveless—"

"Miss Brocas," I corrected him. Brocas was her maiden name, and what little we knew of her past hinted her marriage—to the painter Richard Loveless—may not have been a willing union. "We may get further with her if we address her as such," I explained.

"Appealing to who she was, sir, not who she's become," Jo added at Mr. Smith's frown.

He hesitated, then nodded once. "Point taken, though hopefully this business will not come down to humoring a woman whose reason balances on a knife's edge. Did Windham fill you in about the meetings?" At our nods his frown deepened. "She has been promising the impossible, and many have been foolish enough to accept. There's not a spit of land within several days' sail that is not *someone's* property and thus bounded by laws and restrictions. Yet they're throwing away English citizenship for this fairy tale."

"Not all of us have fared as well as you have, sir," Jo said.

I looked at her in surprise. Her tone was as deferential as ever, but there was a hard gleam in her eye I hadn't seen before. We knew that Mr. Smith was of foreign birth, and he resided with a male lover; yet he was a valued agent of the king, and in all likelihood his position protected them both. But Jo had dear friends at Callisto House, so-called 'unnatural women' who were forced to live apart and under a constant stream of public abuse; too, I had told her of Helena Morrow and the life she had sketched for me, one shaped by the slights of her fellow citizens and the fear of being kidnapped into slavery. I had been insulated from such oppression, not only by the color of my skin but by a father who had loved me unrequitedly and a lover who stood proudly at my side. Countless others had no such protections.

Mr. Smith's cheeks had darkened at her words. Jo paused, letting the moment stretch between them until Mr. Windham let himself in the room. "What have I missed?" he asked.

"Nothing," Mr. Smith snapped, while Jo said mildly, "We were discussing the complication of these passengers. How deeply are they involved? My guess is that Missus Masterson means to use them as fodder, but for all we know they could be acolytes to her cause." She glanced at me.

"Or both," I agreed. "Only it seems strange. To convince them to leave everything behind? Either Miss Brocas is a consummate actor, or she truly believes she is offering them a new life. Only real fervor, I think, could have convinced so many."

"Well, in a few days' time Chase will be able to tell us which it is." Mr. Smith pointed at Jo. "Missus—*Miss Brocas* sails the day after next, and I want you aboard. We'll follow in another ship—"

"Chase and Daniels will be able to tell you," Jo corrected. "Sir."

My heart swelled at her words. I had to duck my head to hide my sudden smile. Beneath the table, she squeezed my hand.

"Don't be absurd," Mr. Smith said. "Miss Brocas has both conversed with and fought Miss Daniels—"

"I gave as good as I got," I interrupted hotly.

"—and will undoubtedly recognize her. It will give the whole game away."

"Of course you did, darling," Jo said to me soothingly, then turned back to Mr. Smith. "Don't worry about Miss Brocas, sir, I'll make sure she doesn't recognize Caroline. But I am afraid it's not up for debate. Either we go together, or we don't go at all."

I was starting to blush when the full import of her words struck me. "How will you keep her from recognizing me?" I asked.

Jo only laid a finger aside her nose, and I bit back a groan.

"Chase," Mr. Windham began, "I know you prefer to work as a team—"

"We cannot take the risk," Mr. Smith cut in.

"Then we shall bid you farewell," Jo said. Her tone had not altered a whit, but her expression had become fixed. "You have several good lads under you. I'm sure you can find one she hasn't clapped eyes on and put him on board."

"For God's sake, Chase. We are all making sacrifices—"

"Yes, we are. Some of us are still in mourning. But Caro

and I *both* know we work better together. If nothing else she keeps me from being rash," Jo added with a grin. "Surely that must be worth some consideration."

Still Mr. Smith hesitated, a multitude of expressions flittering across his features and just as quickly vanishing. Mr. Windham had been watching Jo thoughtfully. Now he said, "I think we should trust their judgment. They have more direct experience with this business than you or I, and I, for one, would feel better with two on board."

Mr. Smith hesitated a moment longer—and then he threw up his hands. "Fine. Both to the ship, but my God, Chase, you keep her away from the Brocas girl. If she gets wind of you we'll be right back where we started. What do you need to pull this off?"

"We sail the day after tomorrow, yes?" At his nod, she grinned again and my stomach fluttered. "Then I will need some money, and conveyance to and from Dormouth."

"Whatever are you up to?" I demanded.

"Wait and see, darling." She leaned over and kissed me. "And just remember, it's all for England."

We settled in our room and rested, for the journey had been wearying. When we rose that evening a dense fog had drifted in, and rather than explore the village we decided to dine at the inn. We were given a snug table by the fire that did much to mitigate the damp. It was lovely to simply converse and enjoy the repast laid before us: an excellent mutton with new potatoes and a parsley sauce, paired with a good French wine. That the latter seemed to be in abundance we did not remark upon, and it amused me to note that when Mr. Smith and Mr. Windham came in, they ordered the same. Serving our king, it seemed, did not extend to enforcing his tariffs.

They did not seek to join us, merely bowed in our direction. I looked to Jo and she shook her head. "Let them talk shop," she murmured, taking my hand. "How are you feeling?"

"Quite content now," I began. "That parsley sauce was wonderful. I wonder if they would share the recipe—"

"I mean about all this."

"Oh." I frowned, thinking. "Well, thus far it seems straightforward: we sail across and report our findings. Though apparently I am to be outlandishly disguised—I can already guess how."

"You cannot blame me for wanting to get you back in breeches," Jo teased. "I haven't seen your lovely legs striding about since Medby."

"Jo!" I gave her a little kick under the table.

"In all seriousness, Caro? It won't be like before." She was playing with my fingers, curling and uncurling them. "Wherever we end up, it won't be English soil. We will be cut off from many resources."

"Then we will simply have to take greater care."

"And you cannot trust Penelope Brocas. I know you want to think the best of her," she pressed as I started to speak. "I know you *believe* her coerced and abused in this. But we don't *know* that, Caro. We must think of her as an enemy until proven otherwise. She would have killed you and Morrow both."

"I know," I murmured. "It's just … I know," I said again, sadly. For all that she had said was true. I had fought Miss Brocas myself, had seen the wildness in her eyes … and yet I couldn't help thinking of her as a trapped animal, lashing out from fear.

"Whether or not you save her, it won't quell your grief, Caro," she whispered. "You have to let that run its course."

And it was all before me then: the loss of my father, my home, everything I had held as certainty in this world—everything except Jo. My eyes welled and Jo quickly dragged her chair around, shielding me from the others' view. "I'm sorry," she breathed. "I'm sorry, darling. That was the wine, making me speak thoughtlessly."

I shook my head, not trusting myself to speak. Jo asked for tea for both of us while I took slow, careful breaths, willing myself calm. A throat cleared in the room, once and then twice. Jo muttered, "what now" and turned, then sucked in her breath. I looked to see what had startled her.

Three women had entered the inn, murmuring apologies for returning late. They were dressed simply, in heavy cloaks and linen dresses, but each wore a scrap of bright white fabric pinned to their cloaks. Somber women, their faces tanned and creased; I glimpsed their rough knuckles and strong hands as each took their key. One leaned heavily on a stout cane as they climbed the stairs, talking in low voices.

I looked at Mr. Smith and he mouthed *ship* and tapped his breast, where the fabric had been pinned. So these were some of Miss Brocas's recruits: three women hoping for something better in life—and leaving everything for a chance at it.

A chance at hope, with the horror of the Leviathan awaiting them. For the first time I truly understood the scope of the Arcadian deception and was overwhelmed with anger and sorrow. I wanted to rush upstairs and tell them all—but would they believe such a fantastic tale? Passage, an offer of land, these things were real; my story was a lurid fiction in comparison. The best we could hope for was to save their lives … and break their hearts in doing so.

My eyes stung once more with tears. When Jo asked me what was wrong, I demurred about wine and exhaustion, and asked to take our tea upstairs. Jo had barely shut the door when I was in her arms, weeping. And bless her, she did not try to make me speak. She just steered me to the bed and held me until I slept.

CHAPTER III

An Unexpected Encounter

I slept remarkably well. Was it the emotions of the previous day, or the wine, or both? I could not say, yet when I awoke I felt refreshed in a way I hadn't for some time. For once, too, Jo had not sprung out of bed at dawn, but was instead sitting up beside me, sipping a cup of tea. Watching her, I felt an overwhelming contentment and burrowed against the curve of her hip. She laid the cup aside and wiggled close in turn, until we were gently twined together … and then we just lay there, drowsing in each other's arms. It all seemed a precious respite, the calm before a storm.

Afterwards, we dressed for our outing to Dormouth. Mr. Windham had left word that the coach was at our disposal. We saw no one we recognized downstairs, either from our own party or any of Miss Brocas's followers. After a light breakfast of toast and eggs we set out on our expedition. I took care to wear both bonnet and scarf, with Jo artfully arranging my hair so it further obscured my face—and stealing a few kisses as she did so.

Again, I marveled at the ships in Dormouth's harbor. Like floating cities, able to go anywhere in the world. We had the coach leave us at the northern end of the bay and began strolling, my hand tucked under Jo's arm. Our plan was to find a purveyor of second-hand clothing, then look for Miss Brocas's ship.

I had given Jo my father's walking stick, the pitted veteran of so many country strolls, and she had polished it to a shine. Its familiar tapping on the cobblestones eased an ache inside me, as if my father was still with us. In the first days after his death, I had realized that grief was no constant, but more like a violent pendulum: now swinging so far away as to resemble a distant memory, now upon me like a wave breaking. Each day the oscillations were a little less wrenching, but only just.

And oh! how he would have thrilled to explore Dormouth: a proper port town, with all the chaos and humanity of such, prettily framed by green and white cliffs. What, I wondered, did newcomers to England think, when their ship worked its way into the harbor and all this appeared before them?

I thought to ask Jo, but she wasn't looking at the landscape. We had come in sight of a market and her eyes were scouring the stalls. Suddenly she steered me through the crowd of shoppers to a stall framed by a striped awning. How she spotted it I could not say, but here we found clothing piled on a table, most of it shabby, some of it smelling unpleasantly of must.

The seller greeted us cordially. Jo explained that my brother was arriving within the week, and we hoped to surprise him with a respectable suit to help him find employment. As she said "respectable," she tapped her coat pocket, making the coins within clink. The man's smile became genuine, and he quickly produced a basket from behind the table. In it were several suits, carefully folded.

"You're about your brother's size," Jo said, a twinkle in her eye. She held up one coat after another before me, finally circling back to a brown suit of good worsted. With a quick glance around, she smoothed the lapels over my bust.

"Jo!" I whispered, willing myself not to blush.

"Coats these days are so fitted, there is not much to let out," she whispered back, grinning at me. "We should err on the side of slightly larger, I think."

When she snapped open the breeches, however, I darted out of reach. "Guess," I told her, turning away—

—only to find myself being stared at by an older man who just as quickly looked down at a tray of fish, but not before I saw his face, tanned to a rich shade of ochre, or the upright posture which with he carried himself. That, and there was a flash of something white on his breast.

Jo surveyed the breeches, measuring the waist with a little smile playing about her lips, then began bartering for the suit. I strolled further away, watching the man, but he made no further attempt to look at me. And why should he? Perhaps he had been staring at something else. Perhaps he had been watching Jo hold the coat up to me, and was ashamed when I caught him.

Perhaps.

I browsed the tables, letting my eyes rove but always looking for that flash of white. Young vegetables, fish so fresh it still seemed to be gasping, an ironmonger banging his pots to show their quality. The man had drifted away without so much as a glance—

—and then I glimpsed an all-too-familiar face.

The woman wore a bonnet as deep as my own, hiding all but the tip of her nose as she argued with a fellow selling canvas. Her delicate brown fingers kept feeling two different bolts, she kept pointing to them in turn and holding a small swatch against each. As she stretched over to touch another bolt, her head turned again, and I once more saw her face.

Helena Morrow did not see me, but I saw her clearly—and the snow-white flower pinned to her breast. Did her brother know she was here, or Mr. Smith? If she were acting as his agent, I felt sure he would have mentioned her. Was she to be on the ship tomorrow? Did her brother know?

"There you are," Jo said, coming up behind me with the bundled suit under her arm. "I got an *excellent* price. We have plenty left for a hat, and perhaps even shoes …"

"Miss Morrow," I whispered.

"*What*? Where?"

At Jo's squawk the bonnet twitched. Quickly I whirled us about to face a woman selling candlewood. "Buying canvas," I whispered. "She hasn't seen me! And she's wearing—" I touched my breast.

Jo looked at me in alarm, then glanced over my shoulder. "I see her," she murmured. "She just handed over a great deal of money for a great deal of canvas."

"Do you think her brother knows?"

"Absolutely not. He never would have brought her into this." Jo's expression was tight with anger. "I don't know what she thinks she's about, but she's on the next coach back to London."

There was an edge to her voice, something more than anger—and then it struck me: Helena was a similar age to

Jo's younger, and now estranged, sister. "Jo," I began carefully, "we don't yet know what she's doing here."

"Clearly she is trying to follow in Morrow's footsteps, without any of his skills—"

"Clear only to you, darling," I put in.

"—and if he finds out she's here, there is no saying how he'll react," she finished.

I started to speak, then hesitated. Though I had more faith in Miss Morrow's abilities, Jo's latter point was important. A reckless, panicked Mr. Morrow might prove disastrous for all our plans.

"Let's follow her," I suggested. It would give us time to think; it would give us time to figure out how to approach this unexpected development. Or so I hoped.

Helena Morrow was a brisk walker. Once her business was concluded she darted away, and it took much doing for Jo and I to keep up with her. Her bonnet was a plain, serviceable grey that resembled a dozen other bonnets at any moment. Jo was still muttering under her breath, phrases like "what is she thinking" and "little fool"; for my part I was focused on not losing her. We passed alehouses and chandleries, dismal inns and even more dismal doorways where women lounged in dishabille. Still, Miss Morrow plunged on.

She led us to the southern end of the bay where a great number of barrels stood upon a pier. We halted at the road, both breathing hard, and pretended to study a noticeboard.

There were a handful of people near the barrels in clothes both well-made and rough, faces dark and pale—but all with some white spot on their breasts, be it a scrap of cloth, a silk flower, or a handkerchief tied through a buttonhole. They greeted Miss Morrow warmly, then indicated the barrels. One was opened and she peered inside, carefully holding herself above the contents. The broad bonnet nodded once, clearly relieving everyone around her. The barrel was sealed once more while a discussion took place, many gesturing towards the bay as they spoke.

"Which ship do you think it is?" I whispered to Jo.

"My guess is the one with the blond figurehead," Jo whispered back. "Europa, or Britannia? It seems a fitting symbol."

I squinted, trying to make out the figureheads despite the sun glinting off the water, and then I saw the ship she meant. It was smaller than the frigate of Thomas Masterson's would-be revolution, and at her bow was the carved figure of a woman, breast bared, golden hair streaming back. Tiny figures were visible on its deck.

"She's leaving," Jo hissed. Indeed, Miss Morrow was bidding the others farewell and turning back towards town—alone. Jo held me back until she was past us, then bodily pulled me after her. "The first quiet corner," she whispered in my ear, "we grab her."

"And do what?" I frowned at her. "Jo, you cannot force her to do anything—"

"I can damn well try," she muttered.

"She is not *your* sister." I laid a hand on her arm, trying to catch her gaze. "And she is a grown woman. We can ask her to explain herself, but little more. And have you considered—" I tugged at her arm— "have you considered that she could get us on that ship?"

At that, Jo finally looked at me, her expression shocked. "You cannot think of using her."

"Not *use* her," I retorted, flushing. "*Align* ourselves with her. And if you weren't so clouded in your judgment right now you would suggest the same."

She looked at me for a beat, and the reproach in her expression—! My mind flew again to her sister Agnes. Oh, that she had stood up to her husband, and kept some contact with Jo! That the very behavior he had held against my darling—dressing as a man, working for Mr. Smith—had begun as an attempt to protect Agnes had mattered not a whit. The papers had been signed, their communication sundered forevermore. I knew it to be another kind of grief, one that Jo had borne stoically until now, but Miss Morrow's presence might bring it back in force.

Ahead of us Miss Morrow turned down a narrow, empty street, and Jo took the opportunity to dart after her, with myself on her heels. I wasn't sure yet if what I proposed was right, but no matter what, Miss Morrow deserved to make her own decisions, and our role was first and foremost to hear her story and apprise her of what we knew.

Halfway down the street, Miss Morrow slowed, and pushed back her bonnet to rub wearily at her face. This seemed all the prompting Jo needed, and with several great steps she bridged the space between them and spun her around. Miss Morrow's face flashed an outrage that swiftly became astonishment. "What are you doing here?" she gasped.

"What are *you* doing here?" Jo retorted. "You're supposed to be in London."

"Not here," I laid a gentle hand on each. "Let us find someplace a little less conspicuous, please."

Jo was rigid beneath my grasp, but Miss Morrow nodded. "We can go to my room, it's the end house." As we fell into step beside her, she asked in a smaller voice, "Does Frannie know?"

"He bloody well should," Jo growled.

"Jo," I admonished. "We will discuss it," I reassured Miss Morrow, smiling at her downcast expression. "I for one would like to hear your story first."

She nodded again, but her expression only became more gloomy. At the last house she unlocked the door, indicating that her room was at the top of the stairs. As she shut the door again, a voice called, "Is that you, Helena?"

"Yes, Missus Lewis. I've come back for a rest, and I have two friends visiting." *How do I introduce you?* she mouthed.

"Mister and Missus Read," I whispered.

"The Reads, Missus Lewis. From London."

A door opened at her words, revealing a middle-aged woman, her skin as dark as deepest night. "How lovely! Are they joining the expedition?"

"We're considering it," I said before Jo could speak.

"If I were twenty years younger, I would be going myself," Mrs. Lewis said. "Only I have a grandchild to mind, and I'm helping my son save for his own boat. But what an adventure! A new land, just for common folk."

My heart sank at her words—and I noticed that Miss

Morrow seemed to be saddened as well, even as she forced a smile and patted the woman's hands. "You're needed here, Missus Lewis," she said soothingly. "And there is no telling what might happen. Why, I might be back on your doorstep in a week's time, asking for more of your excellent stew and help getting back to London."

"Oh, I doubt it. But you know you're always welcome." She smiled at us. "How about a nice pot of tea? I can bring it up to you."

"You are too kind! That would be much appreciated," I said, pushing Jo up the stairs.

Miss Morrow's room was surprisingly airy for such a small house, with a partial view of the bay past the surrounding rooftops. There was a bed, a chest of drawers topped with a washbasin, and a little table and chair. Jo and I had a swift, silent battle over the seating, in which she wanted to remain standing while I took the chair; but I knew looming over the poor woman would do more harm than good, and I bodily pushed her down into the chair and settled on the bed while leaving space for Miss Morrow.

"Where are my manners?" Miss Morrow exclaimed as she entered the room. "Give me your things, please. I can ask to use the sitting room—"

"But we might be overheard," I said. "This is fine, Miss Morrow, truly. Now please, sit down and tell us how you came to be here."

And for a moment I thought perhaps Jo had the right of it, for the woman who sat down beside me seemed to wither as she did so, becoming more frightened girl than decisive adult. "I don't know where to begin," she said. "It all happened so quickly—is Frannie here?"

"He may well come, once he finds out," Jo said ominously.

"But he's not supposed to travel!" she cried. "The doctor thinks it will bring on the fever again."

I arched my eyebrows at Jo: *well?* She wrinkled her nose, but I saw her relax imperceptibly. "Point taken, Miss Morrow. We were not aware that his health was still fragile. I'm sure we can resolve this between ourselves."

We were interrupted by Mrs. Lewis knocking and bringing in the tea-tray. "Should I pour?" she asked.

"I can pour," I said. "Thank you for this."

"Well. If you need anything else," she said, and withdrew once more.

We all three waited, listening to her receding steps, the door to the kitchen opening and closing; only then did I pour three cups of tea, and at Miss Morrow's murmured assent added milk and sugar. Jo took her cup and looked Miss Morrow in the eye.

"We can resolve this," she repeated. "Just start at the beginning and tell us everything."

CHAPTER IV

Families

"I never intended to come this far," Miss Morrow began. Her voice was catching. At my urging, she took a sip of her tea and when she spoke again, she was calmer. "I have been going to meetings of the Ladies' Anti-Slavery Society for many weeks now. I helped my mother nurse Frannie those first days after we brought him home, but once his fever broke, I was eager to resume my attendance ... and the very first night I went, Penelope was there! As if nothing had happened, as if she had not tried to murder my brother!

"She was disguised, but only just, and she freely gave her name to any who asked. I could not believe it. I thought at any moment someone would come to seize her. But she sat through the meeting as calm as could be, and afterwards began talking to people about a self-governing colony called Arcadia, not two days' sail from England. I knew the name from those paintings. I drew close, thinking to do *something ...*" Miss Morrow looked from myself to Jo. "And then she recognized me."

"She knew you for Morrow's sister?" Jo exclaimed.

"No! She knew me as an *artist*." Her voice nearly broke again. "She remembered me from a sketching class, just after her marriage to Richard Loveless. He came to give us a demonstration and she had accompanied him and admired my work. That night at the meeting she appealed to me as a fellow artist, one who could help her finish an unusual commission."

"So you blithely agreed to help her," Jo snapped before I could hush her.

"I thought I could help *you*," Miss Morrow retorted, her chin raising. "Clearly your Mister Smith had lost her, and here she was inviting me to work closely with her. My first thought was to ascertain her plans and convey them to Frannie, but his recovery has been so fraught, and I worried he would do something foolish. So I decided instead to report to Mister Smith directly ... and collect the payment myself," she finished in a smaller voice.

I leaned forward and steadied Miss Morrow's hands, which were making her teacup shiver. "The money is important, I take it," I said gently.

Her cheeks darkened at my words. "Difficulties have a way of, of *accumulating*, Miss Daniels. My father's health is declining and my parents face much competition now. On every street there seem to be new, larger shops of every description. For some months our bills have outnumbered our profits. I had not realized to what extent my parents had come to rely on Frannie's payments from Mister Smith, or how outrageous a sum he had been promised for bringing Missus Masterson to justice—a sum he had conveyed to my parents, who then placed orders as if the money was a certainty. We had to use part of my dowry to pay for our last shipment of goods. I have said nothing to poor Gerald," she continued in a quieter voice. "He thinks I am visiting a friend, and we are still to marry next year. But my commissions earn shillings, not guineas."

Again, I looked at Jo, who had relaxed fully, the anger and worry in her face replaced by sympathy. "Your motives are admirable, Miss Morrow, and both Caro and I are familiar with such struggles," she said. "But now you understand how quickly one can become cornered in these affairs. It's precisely why your brother coordinates his efforts with Mister Smith and Mister Windham."

Miss Morrow nodded. "At the time I truly believed Arcadia was just a story, perhaps a way to raise funds. She invited me to walk with her the following day, which we spent discussing painting techniques. Specifically, techniques for enlarging a preliminary drawing, such as to cover ceilings or walls—or canvases of unusual size."

Now Jo was leaning forward as well, her face bright with alarm. "Unusual size?" she prodded.

"I tried to get her to describe this commission, but she would say little; I think she was testing me." Miss Morrow shook her head. "I'm still not certain what she intends, and it seemed foolish to go to Mister Smith with so little to relate. And then …"

She trailed off, her lip trembling. "And then," I prompted.

"She invited me to meet her again. I thought she intended another discussion about painting, so I agreed. But instead, I found myself at a gathering … there were so many people there, of every race and creed. She was speaking to them of Arcadia, and they were so *hopeful* …" She paused again, taking a breath to steady her voice. "Several of them told me their stories. About losing work, losing spouses to illness or prison. About how they were on the brink of calamity. Until Penelope offered them Arcadia." She looked at us somberly. "This is the third, and final, ship. She has given each person free passage and a piece of land, merely on the promise that they will lay down their lives to protect Arcadia. There are already dozens of people on that island—"

"Or dozens murdered by the monster," Jo put in.

Her words brought Miss Morrow up short, and then the first tears began winding down her cheeks. "I didn't know what to do," she said in a trembling voice. "I was afraid if I went to Mister Smith those poor people might be arrested. I could not live with myself if that happened."

I gave her my handkerchief, but my eyes were on Jo. She spread her hands and shook her head; as flummoxed as I, it seemed, on how to proceed.

When Miss Morrow's weeping had subsided, I asked, "Have you learned anything else?"

"I believe Missus Masterson is on this island, wherever it is," she replied in a shuddering voice. "Penelope read a dispatch from her at that gathering, describing in detail improvements being made there."

"Could she have found some uninhabited island and claimed it for herself?" I asked Jo.

"It is possible," Jo replied thoughtfully. "But even so, I doubt that's the limit of her ambitions. She is planning to wield the monster once more, I'm certain of it—the monster and its brood."

I nodded, pondering Jo's words—and then I remembered.

"What was in the barrels you were inspecting?" I asked Miss Morrow.

"Varnish. For sealing canvas."

"But no rotting fish?"

She recoiled at my words. "Rotting fish? Why would there be rotting fish?"

"Your brother didn't tell you?" At her headshake I gave Jo a pointed look: *see?* "Miss Brocas had a jar of what appeared to be rotting fish in her studio," I explained. "We thought perhaps she mixed it into the paint to create the, the doorway. If, say, it was a small piece of the Leviathan—? I know little of witchcraft, but I know one of its principles is like to like—say, using a person's hair to hex them. Perhaps this is similar."

"Or a lot of superstitious rubbish," Jo said, "and it means little for our circumstances, even if true." She was gazing at Miss Morrow with what seemed merely a thoughtful expression; only I knew the tension in her jaw spoke of greater emotions being held in check. "I don't want you to risk yourself further," she said to Miss Morrow. "But I think we must keep to our plan. Once we have seen Arcadia for ourselves, we can act swiftly. Can you help us get on that ship, and then go to Smith and tell him what you told us?"

Miss Morrow's brow furrowed again. I sipped my tea. When Jo looked at me I gave a little shake of my head. This was her decision alone.

"I can get you on board," she said at last. "But I am coming as well." Before either of us could object she continued, "Penelope is—she is not right in her mind, and many innocent people are in danger. If I stay by her side, I can vouch for you both, and try to steer her towards reasonableness. If she tries to use the paintings to conjure the monster, I might be able to undermine her efforts. And I am familiar to the others. They may listen to me should matters come to crisis."

Jo was shaking her head. "It is far too risky—"

"The risk does not figure, Miss Chase. I have no choice." She looked at Jo, her eyes welling once more. "If I don't go, and the worst happens, how am I to live with myself? Tell me that and I will stay."

"It wouldn't be your fault," Jo snapped. "You are not to blame for any of this."

"No, I'm not. But I can help stop it; I may be uniquely placed to stop it. So again, I ask you: how am I to live with myself if I abandon these people?"

Jo fell silent. My heart ached for the warring emotions on her face, but I knew too that what Miss Morrow said was true.

"If that is your decision, then so be it," I said. "But if we are to work together—and our odds are much improved by our doing so, I think you can see that—I must make two requests of you. One, if you cannot get us on board, do not go without us. We will try a different approach, together. And two, if we do manage to get on board, you stay as close as you can to us, and you respond to our cues without hesitation. We will have knowledge that you will not," I pressed when she started to speak. "We'll be receiving instructions from Mister Smith—instructions that must also be yours, no matter how they may seem in the moment."

Miss Morrow nodded. "Agreed," she said, and there was newfound vigor in her voice.

"What do you need from us?"

"To be here at daybreak," she said promptly. "I will try to add you to the manifest, but if that fails, we may have to resort to subterfuge."

"You say that so calmly," I said, smiling.

"My brother has demonstrated all manner of skulduggery over the years," she replied, smiling as well. "He also taught me to protect myself. Do not fear that I lack ability."

At the mention of Mr. Morrow, Jo visibly flinched, and I touched her knee. I could not read her thoughts, but I knew well that she was unhappy. "Then perhaps we should depart—"

"May I also ask a concession of you?" Jo asked, her voice soft. At Miss Morrow's nod she continued, "May I ask that you write to your brother and your parents?"

The question brought Miss Morrow up short. Her cheeks darkened again. "If Frannie learns I'm here, he is bound to come, and he's not supposed to travel."

"Miss Morrow, this undertaking will put us all in mortal danger." Jo was choosing her words carefully. Beneath my hand I could feel her trembling, though her voice was steady. "If you are killed in this, they will spend their lives wondering: why did she go, could we have saved her? A word from you now would give them comfort should the worst come to pass."

Miss Morrow ducked her head. "I—I hadn't thought," she whispered, audibly swallowing. "You are right. You are absolutely right. I will write at once."

"If you send it to our inn, we can add it to the London dispatch. That would ensure it arrives."

"You are right," she repeated. "I will do so."

There seemed no more to say then. In that somber mood we donned our coats and cloaks, hats and bonnets, and I took up the bundled suit. I bid Miss Morrow farewell and she impulsively hugged me, crushing the garments between us. For a moment I held her slight, trembling body in my arms, but when we broke apart she was smiling too brightly. "I understand Miss Chase's sentiment," she said, "but I am certain we will prevail in this."

"Of course we will." I looked to Jo for confirmation, but she was already gone.

"Have I—have I upset her?"

"It's not you." I patted her arm. "You were an unexpected surprise is all. She will be fine in the moment, never fear."

As I turned to leave Miss Morrow said, "Tomorrow, what names shall I use? Mister and Missus Read?"

I paused at the door, trying to think. "No, I will be disguised ... and I think Miss Brocas knows the name Daniels. Put us down as Mister Simmons and Mister Read," I finished. It would have to do. With a last nod I took my leave of her, though I knew I would hold in my heart always that last glimpse of her: slight yet resolute, her chin raised even though fresh tears were clinging to her lashes.

Outside, Jo was standing some ways down the street. When I went to her, she would not meet my eyes until I turned her towards me.

"Jo, she will be all right," I began. "We will both look out for her—"

"I keep thinking," Jo cut in, "how I would feel if she were Agnes and I was in Morrow's shoes. To have no say in her fate, to not even speak to her, before …" She shook her head. I saw then she was on the verge of tears. "Yes, this is the *sensible* plan; it may even be the only plan. But it's not *right*."

"Jo," I began again, but words failed me. None of it was right, but what else could we do? So many lives were at stake.

"Could you take the coach back?" she asked. "I—I just want to walk back alone. I need some air; I need to think."

As she spoke, I felt as if I had been plunged into icy water, so nerveless did my body become. I knew it was an innocuous request; I knew too how it felt to be caught in a surge of grief. Yet I suddenly felt cold and panicked, in a way I never had before.

"Don't go," I whispered. "At least—at least ride back with me?" There was a note of fear in my voice that seemed to come from some other Caroline. What did we have to fear? We were in a populous town at midday, and Miss Brocas had but glimpsed Jo the once. Yet the thought of Jo walking off, alone, made my heart race. "You could walk the pier in Dormouth," I added quickly when she hesitated. "You could walk the pier, and then we can talk over supper, as we always do."

She looked at me with an unreadable expression, then squeezed my hand. "Of course," she murmured. "Of course, darling."

"We'll figure it out," I continued in a rush. "I promise." Inwardly I winced at my own words, at their neediness, but my heart was still racing. I felt as if I was standing upon a precipice—

Again she nodded, and sensation flooded back into my limbs at her simple acquiescence. As I raised my arm to signal the coach she blurted out, "But your hat—we were going to buy you a hat."

"Oh, bother my hat," I cried. I waved vigorously to the coach, nearly striking two passing men as I did so. I was almost trembling as Jo helped me inside. Not until the door had shut and she was snugly beside me did I feel that strange, fluttering terror inside me start to quiet. A tightness in my chest loosened, though I had not realized I was experiencing such, and my racing heartbeat slowed. All at the mere thought of her walking alone. What then of Arcadia, what if I faltered and lost us both?

I would not, I would not. My hands, buried in the crumpled suit, curled into fists. Jo had promised we would decide together, act together; I would be her equal partner in courage. I would master myself for her sake. I had to. There was no turning back now, not with Miss Morrow involved.

And it was not until we were halfway back to Dormouth that I remembered: the two men I had nearly struck both had white scraps pinned to their lapels; that, and one of them had been the man from the marketplace. But when I started to tell Jo, I saw she was lost in her own unhappy thoughts, her eyes shimmering, and instead I simply pressed against her, trying to give us both what comfort I could.

Upon our return, Jo went down to the pier after first giving me a searching look. My smile must have reassured her, though I could muster no true emotion behind it. Inside the inn, I turned down Mr. Windham's invitation to dine, claiming a need for rest, though I asked him for help finding a hat and he promised to procure something suitable. At the stairs, Mr. Smith asked me if we needed anything else and I thanked him. Jo would certainly speak to him if she thought of something—

And there I stopped myself, lest I suddenly blurt out *no more, I cannot do this, you must fend for yourselves.* I had been given ample opportunities to turn his request down. Now, knowing of Miss Morrow and the others? How could I refuse, no matter the risk?

In our room I flung myself down on the bed, feeling drained in a way I had not felt since my father's funeral. Then, it had been grief overwhelming me; now I set myself to understanding where this sudden terror had come from, and how I might rid myself of it. I had known all along that we were risking our lives, as did Jo. Indeed, she had written her own letter to Agnes, should the worst come to pass, and I had written to the Simmonses. All through those preparations I had felt certain in our decision, certain that it was our duty to end this horror. The presence of Miss Morrow had merely put a dear face to the threat the monster posed.

And then it struck me, with such force it left me breathless: I did not fear dying, I feared *surviving.* I feared that I would *survive* Jo. That she would be gone and I would have to carry on, alone.

The very thought—oh! It felt as if I were staring into an

abyss. My heartbeat quickened and my breath caught in my throat, just as they had outside Miss Morrow's lodgings. I tried to reason with myself: we had faced these odds before, our only task was to gather information, Mr. Smith's ship would be nearby. But while my mind could review our circumstances calmly, my body reacted as if we were in terrible peril—even in the quiet of the inn. What, then, might happen when we landed in Arcadia? My fear could prove deadly.

Had I ever felt such terror before? Certainly, I had been given cause to fear since Edward Masterson first came into our lives, but this felt different—more instinctive, more physical. Before then, my only truly fearful memory was of my mother's passing when I had witnessed what no child should see: all the blood of that torturous birth, her stricken, contorted body, and Mrs. Simmons and the midwife dressing my stillborn brother. I had been unable to scream, I had been unable to move, I had become this *seeing* thing—

And then my father had forcibly turned me away and said through his own tears, *Caroline, Caroline. Breathe, that's my girl. In and out, in and out. That's my girl.* He had laid his warm, comforting hand upon my chest and nodded encouragingly at every rise and fall. And I had obeyed, breathing in time with his instructions, until my own tears came at last.

Now I laid my hand upon my chest as he had done, and I took one shuddering breath after another. *In and out, in and out.* In my mind's eye it was not my hand's pressure I felt but his own, its very presence making me feel safe and loved. With each breath my heartbeat slowed; beneath the weight of my hand the tightness in my chest lessened. *That's my girl.* When I finally wept it was like a dam bursting: the past pouring into the present, tainting the future before us.

"Caroline," a voice whispered in my ear.

I roused myself with difficulty. At first, I could not focus, so dark was the room, and then Jo's pallid, worried face swam into view. I smiled reassuringly before I could even think. *Breathe, that's my girl.* "Are you all right?" she whispered.

"I was overwrought," I admitted. "I must have fallen asleep … what time is it?"

"Late enough that our supper is cold." She was still looking worried. "Caro, if you don't feel up to this—"

"I'm all right." Or at least I would be; I had to be. I wiped at my face, twisted my hair into some semblance of order. "I think it was our conversation with Miss Morrow. It is one thing to know the risks, another to put a face to them."

A true enough statement, though not the whole truth; still the worry left Jo's face, replaced by a weary sympathy. "She is as stubborn as her brother," she said with a sigh. "I only wish she was as devious."

"She may yet surprise us. Have you been walking all this time?"

"Not exactly." She took a tray with two plates of sausages and potatoes from the table—had she brought it up? How long had I slept?—and laid it on my lap before climbing into bed next to me. "I wrote to Morrow, and I spoke to Smith about her."

That simple report, delivered in a breath—oh, what would

Miss Morrow have said to it? We had not discussed telling either about her presence. But it was done now, for better or worse. I handed her one of the plates as I asked, "What did Mister Smith say?"

"Well, he hasn't scuppered our plans, in case you were hoping. He is actually pleased, can you believe it? He thinks Morrow sent her here to keep his hand in. Wouldn't hear of changing anything. The man would throw us all to the wolves if it helped his cause." She laughed bitterly. "If we survive this, you and I really must find another way to earn our daily bread."

If we survive this. "Agreed," I said, thankful my voice sounded normal. I cut a piece of sausage, chewed the cold meat, swallowed. *Breathe, that's my girl.* "Should you have written to Mister Morrow?" I continued. "His sister will, I'm certain of it."

Jo ate a forkful of cold potato with a grimace. "As am I. But I wanted him to know that we will look out for her. That we *are* looking out for her." She took a shuddering breath. "As I walked, I kept thinking, what would I want, if it were Agnes? And there were many things, but this, at least, was a thing I could *do* ... since apparently I am not allowed to bundle her onto the first coach to London."

For a moment I let myself imagine it: all three of us on a coach, not looking back. "We need to get on that ship," I said, as much for my own benefit as hers.

"Shove her over the side just as we're drawing away?" she asked hopefully.

I smiled at that, a real smile. "Jo! She would hate you—"

"She would be alive to hate me."

"—and she was right. You know it as well as I. She is uniquely placed." At her downcast expression I nudged her. "She showed not a hint of hesitation or fear." Which was more than could be said for myself. "If she had, then you and I would be working out how to get her off the boat tomorrow, not how to get on."

Jo nudged me back. "I told you, we just toss her over the side. There will be dozens to help her out of the drink."

"I was thinking a more ladylike distraction: we send her back to fetch something, then sail away before she can return."

"Always making things complicated." But she suddenly laid her plate aside. "Oh Caro," she whispered, "I don't feel good about any of this. I cannot tell if it's instinct, or that she reminds me of Agnes, or lingering grief over your father, or …"

And there it was again: that wondrous sympathy between us—yet to admit to my own fears might make us both falter. I put the tray at the foot of the bed, then turned to her, trying to smile. "In Medby you told me *we will survive this*, and we did. So I tell you now, Jo Chase: we are three brave, intelligent women, and we will survive this."

But Jo didn't respond. She only hugged me, burying her face in my neck, and I hugged her back as tightly as I could. *In and out, in and out.* I cannot say how long we stayed in our embrace, each locked in our own fears, together and yet separate. Finally, we moved the plates to the floor and curled up together, and I was insensible until dawn.

CHAPTER V

Setting Off

We awoke at dawn and dressed in silence, Jo helping me to bind my breasts, I lacing her jumps snug. In front of our door was a worn tricorn hat, with a note in Mr. Windham's handwriting: *good luck to you both.* We did not speak, save that our touches lingered, that we paused sometimes to plant the briefest kisses on bare skin, not gestures of affection or desire, but putting a seal to promises made. *Together.* To speak would somehow make it all real; to speak would be to bring back all our fears in force. For those few minutes, the thin sunlight slowly bringing the world to life around us, we were united in silent accord to keep at bay all that was to come.

Jo strapped a knife to my forearm, then drew my sleeve down over it. The rigid form against my arm felt strange, yet better that than a pistol, for I knew my aim to be middling at best. Thus it was Jo who tucked our pistol into her breeches before strapping a knife to her own arm. She combed my hair and gathered it into a bourse, and I combed hers in turn and tied it back, relishing its thick softness. With sure, practiced movements she painted her face, adding a hint of fuzz above her lip and deepening the shadows around her eyes. And then she held up a finger, and after rummaging in her bag produced a familiar pair of thick-framed spectacles: the same that she had used to disguise herself at Medby. The sight of them, so innocuous and yet so laden with memory, brought a fresh pang of grief. I had to blink back sudden tears as she balanced them on my nose.

"The lenses are plain glass, remember?" She took a step back, surveying the result of her handiwork. "But they should confound Miss Brocas, should it come to that."

I looked at myself in the small, speckled mirror. How strange I appeared, with my hair bundled up, my breasts bound, and the spectacles obscuring my face! I took the lenses off, then put them back on again. Jo was right; without them I was a close relation of Caroline Daniels, but with them on I seemed another person entirely, a nondescript young man of little means.

"Darling, you are brilliant," I said, and to my delight, she blushed.

"They were the first thing I thought of when we decided to come south." She wrapped her arms around me. "There was no way I was letting that bloody woman—"

"Language," I admonished.

"—have another go at you." She nuzzled my neck. "You look most fetching, Mister—did we choose names?"

"I told Miss Morrow that we would be Mister Simmons and Mister Read."

"Which one will I be? I have to say, I much prefer you as Mister Read, for I rather fancy him …"

Her hands started to roam as we kissed, the spectacles jostling between us. "With your genius at work," I said when we broke apart, "I believe not only will we survive this, we might even come out quite well."

"Come away with me if we do?" Jo asked, and though she was smiling her eyes were serious.

"Come away? Come away where?"

"Anywhere." She gestured vaguely. "I was thinking on it, last night … if we do succeed, if we truly end this? The reward will be substantial, Caro. We could go wherever we pleased, see more of the world. Perhaps find someplace where it's easier to be … us."

And I could see it, then: a village or even a town where there was never any hesitation in greeting us, never any whispers behind our backs; where we never had to fear pamphlets on our doorstep, or the stocks, or worse; where we did not have to risk our lives just to feed ourselves …

"Yes," I said, though my throat was tight. "Yes."

She embraced me then, and in that moment it all felt possible: arresting Mrs. Masterson, destroying the monster, saving Miss Morrow, all the Arcadia-bound innocents, and even Penelope Brocas. In that moment, I would have bet everything I had on us: on our intelligence, our courage, our love.

The morning light cast a peaceful glow over Dormouth's streets, but already there were many people going about their business. Dinghies were being loaded and unloaded, shopkeepers were sweeping their front steps, and we could hear the cries of the market. Miss Brocas's ship floated placidly in the bay, but there was a dinghy alongside and crates were being winched on board.

We disembarked near Miss Morrow's lodgings, Jo shouldering the one satchel we were bringing. On top were the items for show: two changes of linen, a razor, our papers, and a small Bible Jo had procured from somewhere with the same flourish as my spectacles—the trappings of two poor young men making their way in the world. Buried underneath, however, was Jo's little pot of makeup, a telescope, and a lantern with thick, distended glass, which Mr. Smith had assured us would be bright enough to be seen across a distance, such as from the Arcadian shore to another ship lying in wait. He and Mr. Windham had calculated an approximate area for the island, a spot on the map avoided by most vessels due to its swirling tides and recurring fog. They planned to anchor at the next closest island, and if Jo and I could make it to the northern end of Arcadia, and use the lantern with its special lenses, and if the fog wasn't too dense—

If, if. And now we had a deadline too, as a result of Jo's conference with him: after two days, if there was no word, Mr. Smith would simply annex the island with the blunt weapon that was our Navy. If our destination was indeed where he and Mr. Windham believed, we would arrive tomorrow morning, *Saturday* morning. If we did not signal, he would take the island by force on Monday. We simply had to survive that long ... and talk dozens of Arcadians out of keeping their word to Miss Brocas.

But I tried not to think on the ifs. Instead, I held to that conviction I had felt at the inn, the vision of our lives as they might be. *Breathe.* I thought on it as we sent the coach back and made our way to Miss Morrow's door; I thought on it as Jo raised her hand to knock, only to have the door opened promptly by a bright-eyed Miss Morrow. She touched her lips, then pointed at an upstairs window. We waited while she locked the door behind her, then put the key through the letter-box. Only when she had led us down the street a ways did she pause to rummage in her own satchel.

"Good morning," she said in a quiet voice. Deftly she tied a scrap of white cloth through a buttonhole on each of our coats. Her own silk flower stood out vividly against the dark wool of her cloak.

"Good morning to you," I replied, while Jo said, "Good morning, and how fare our prospects of boarding?"

"Strangely excellent," she murmured. With a glance up and down the street she continued, "I told Penelope last night I had spoken with two young men interested in Arcadia, that you had no real prospects here in England and had been considering trying your luck abroad … and she promptly declared that it was my *duty* to make sure you both came—? It was almost as if she were referring to someone else." She frowned. "She was not herself last night. She came down to inspect the cargo, but then she hardly looked at anything. She was terribly pale, and thinner than I had seen her last. I could not be certain she truly recognized me or understood what I was saying to her."

"Could it be the strain?" Jo asked. "Or, dare I say, con-science?"

"Strain, certainly. Conscience, I cannot speak to." But

there was a tremor in her voice as she spoke, and I laid a hand on her arm.

"Is there something—" I began.

"She just seems so frail," Miss Morrow blurted out. "I cannot reconcile her with Frannie's injuries. There are times when she appears too weak to walk, much less wield a weapon."

"And yet she was that person," I said gently. "I understand your sentiments, and indeed I share them to an extent. She is very young, and it's possible she was coerced into this affair. But it does not change what she did, Miss Morrow, and you must act as if she could do it again, at any moment."

Miss Morrow nodded, but said more softly, "We are the same age, Miss Daniels."

"And think what you might be capable of, in terrible circumstances."

She hesitated at that, then nodded again, this time with more resolve, and resumed her brisk walk towards the bay. Jo and I quickened our pace to meet Miss Morrow's; her natural gait seemed to be a purposeful stride that moved unerringly towards its goal.

"I think now is a good time for us to discuss a cruder topic," she said. "I want to ensure we understand each other before we sail. Whatever payment there is to be had for undermining Missus Masterson's plot, it will be a three-way split."

Jo snorted with amusement, and I nearly laughed myself. "I think an equable division is fair to all involved, Miss Morrow," I said. "What terms you work out with your brother, however, I leave to your discretion."

"Terms with Frannie?" She looked at us in astonishment,

not once breaking stride. "This is all for our parents! He doesn't get a penny."

"Not even for passage to France?" Jo's tone was sly, and I elbowed her hard. We had no way of knowing what, if anything, Mr. Morrow had told his family about his sojourn there. Certainly, broaching that he had taken a French mistress could make for an uncomfortable conversation.

And perhaps it was my fault, then, for letting my thoughts go to that woman, for just at that moment Miss Morrow exclaimed, "That reminds me! I remembered something last night, after you left. Frannie had mentioned something about a French spy helping him with the Masterson investigation. He kept saying she had 'gone ahead,' that she was 'there already.' It was one of the reasons he was so upset at being bedridden. He was in contact with her, though he did not want to inform Mister Smith—he kept referring to her as the ace up his sleeve. But if she's already on Arcadia she may be able to help us."

Jo looked at me then, rolling her eyes; I spread my hands helplessly. "Was her name perhaps Viart?" Jo asked.

"Oh yes! Madame Viart. You know her, then? Well, of course you would, having worked with Frannie before." She smiled. "Then our circumstances are better than I thought. If she's there, we can make contact right away."

"Oh, we know her all right," Jo said with a groan. "Leave it to Morrow to get his—" I elbowed her again, hard enough that she yelped.

"His what?" Miss Morrow looked from Jo to myself, frowning.

"His fee up. Once he made contact with her, he could charge Mister Smith for two, you see." I spoke in a rush. When I gave Jo a look, she nodded vigorously.

Miss Morrow studied our faces a moment longer, clearly suspicious, before looking ahead once more. "Bloody Viart," Jo whispered in my ear, but I could only muster a weak smile in response. Oh, anyone but Madame Viart! In Medby I had placed myself in her debt to save Jo's life and I had no doubt that in these dire circumstances she would be quick to call in that particular chit. I had asked Jo for a promise, that we would make our decisions together. I had not reckoned that I might be the one who struggled to keep it.

CHAPTER VI
Into the Unknown

J was nervous as we approached the bay, but the bustle of preparations eased my fears. Just as Miss Morrow had described, there were people from all walks of life talking and shouting in an uproarious din, and we swiftly blended in with the throng. Miss Morrow led us to an assortment of crates, atop which were the bundles of canvas she had purchased. After a quick conference we each took one, all three of us grimacing at the weight, and followed Miss Morrow to one of the waiting dinghies. She spoke to the two burly, tanned sailors manning the boat and then waved us close. There were already two other women and a man waiting, the women sitting down. Miss Morrow joined them and I nearly climbed in myself when I remembered my persona. Instead, Jo and I added our bundles to the goods inside, took off our shoes and stockings, and helped push the boat out into the cold water. The sheer effort strained muscles I did not know I had and I nearly fell in the process, but the others regarded my struggles with a friendly sympathy, not suspicion.

As the sailors began rowing, one of the women pointed. "There's Miss Brocas!" she cried. "Miss Brocas! Hello!"

I followed the pale line of her arm and saw, for the first

time in weeks, Penelope Brocas. But this was not the ragged creature we had dragged back through the painting. The woman on the pier was standing erect, her blond hair streaming soft and loose around her, her dress immaculately white from head to toe. Yet what would have appeared angelic in another context seemed ominous here, like a poisoned flower. That bright whiteness, so often a sign of innocence and goodness, made Miss Brocas appear ghostly, more apparition than flesh-and-blood woman. As she approached the water's edge, people rushed up to her, some clasping her hands, others touching her dress with unsettling reverence.

"Oh, I wish we had taken the next boat," the woman said fretfully. "I wanted to speak with her."

"She'll be sailing with us, Annie." The man patted her hand with his own large, whitish paw, two of his fingers severed at the first knuckle from some longago accident. "You'll get your chance, I'm sure of it."

The other woman leaned towards us, a keen expression on her face. "You have both taken the vow, then?"

The phrase startled me, though I managed to conceal my surprise. Miss Morrow had spoken of a vow to protect Arcadia. Was this what she had meant? I wanted to reply but dared not—my voice was too high—but Jo said, "Indeed we have. A fellow wants something to commit to in life." The man murmured a soft *hear hear* as Jo continued, with a nod towards Miss Morrow, "We are indebted to our friend for convincing us. She works closely with Miss Brocas."

At once their attention swiveled to Miss Morrow. "Have you served her long?" the first woman, Annie, asked. "She must be a wonderful mistress."

Hurt flash briefly across Miss Morrow's face. "I am assisting Miss Brocas with her paintings," she replied. "I am a trained painter and engraver."

Her words in turn visibly confused Annie. But what was the confusion? I remembered the pride in Miss Morrow's voice: *She knew me as an artist.* Did she always face such disbelief in her talents?

"You're welcome to live with us until you get your house," the man was saying to Jo. "My brother has been there for some time now. He got one of the first cottages, right by the green."

"They're building so quickly?" Jo asked.

"Building?" The other woman laughed. "Did they not explain? The houses were already built. A whole village, just waiting for people to fill it again. Miss Brocas said it was a miracle."

As she spoke, I was filled with an icy dread. A miracle, or an act of evil? A village's worth of people would keep the monster sated for some time.

"I heard that, but I could not believe it," Jo said. "How could such a thing be?"

"Missus Masterson thinks perhaps sickness drove the earlier folks to leave," the man said. "Not quite a miracle—" This he delivered with an admonishing look at the other woman "—but the houses are just sitting there, the soil is good, there's fish in the water … it would be a sin to leave the place uninhabited."

"And she's been there how long?"

"Oh, a couple years now. When did our Philip go out there?" He looked at Annie.

"Over a year now," Annie said. "Right after Christmas before last. We thought him foolish, sailing in winter like that, with nothing but a handshake and a slip of paper! Now look at us."

"It was just a few people at first, folks who were known to Missus Masterson," the man explained. "Right after she inherited the island."

A couple years ago—! Back then Edward Masterson had been feeding his wives to the Leviathan and taking their money for himself. Had it been to finance this scheme? An island between England and France, ruled by neither. How had it come to the Masterson family?

But that was a question for afterwards; what mattered now was what Mrs. Masterson was planning, and how we could stop her.

We reached the ship. Our goods were hauled up, then the women helped on board. Jo and I followed, clambering up a ladder. Again my body ached, for when had I climbed so? It was with relief that I felt hands seize my arms and help me over the side.

And then I found myself face-to-face with the man from the marketplace.

This time there was no embarrassment or aversion. He looked strangely satisfied, as if my arrival were expected. By the time I found my footing on deck he had melted into the crowd—but no, there he was, conversing with a knot of men.

Again, I thought to say something to Jo, but we were being greeted by a dozen others, all congratulating us on joining this great enterprise, all with something white on their breasts. There was excited talk about building schemes, designating land for pasture, ways to monetize the excellent fishing. Someone pointed back towards the shore where two more boats were rowing out. In one was Miss Brocas, sitting upright in the stern, the sunlight glinting off her hair. A woman's voice began singing

There is a land of pure delight,
where Saints immortal reign;
infinite day excludes the night,
and pleasures banish pain.

And soon the whole ship was singing, their voices carrying back to the pier where I saw sailors and laborers turn in surprise. Jo moved closer to me, her hand tucked into the opposite cuff where I knew she was touching the knife's handle for reassurance. I looked at Miss Morrow; she was mouthing the words but gave me a little shake of her head, seemingly as unnerved as we were.

Could we but climb where Moses stood,
and view the landscape o'er,
not Jordan's stream, nor death's cold flood,
should fright us from the shore!

Miss Brocas's dinghy drew alongside. Their goods were lifted up and then she was raised onto the ship in a sling, glowing white and yellow. I put on my spectacles, keeping my face slightly averted for good measure. Though she still resembled that longago portrait we had seen in London, up close I saw a new gauntness to her frame. Had she grown even thinner than when we struggled on that otherworldly beach? The gaze that flitted over us was hollow; the smile that twisted her lips seemed a chilling rictus. As she began making her way towards us, Jo bowed and tugged me down beside her, so all we saw of her was a cloud of white skirts.

"Helena," she said in a quavering voice. "Will you sit with me a while?"

I nearly looked up, so childish and needy did she sound, but Jo coughed and I stayed bent over. Miss Morrow assented and then, under pretense of adjusting her skirts, ducked her head beside Jo's. "Bring the canvases to the hold," she whispered. "I will meet you there."

And then she was gone, following the golden glimmering swirl of Penelope Brocas towards the quarterdeck and its galleries.

"She seems strained," Jo murmured, straightening beside me.

"She seems about to collapse," I replied, matching her tone.

"Isn't she lovely?" We turned to see the man we had sailed with. "A proper angel is Miss Brocas. Would that we had her like on the throne, we wouldn't have to leave."

"Better than those Hanovers," Annie muttered. "What right do they have to rule us?"

"Hush now," he admonished her. "We're a bit more forthright in the north," he said to us with an apologetic smile. "Come on, Annie. Let's make ourselves comfortable."

We inclined our heads as they went to the hold. "We have canvas to bring below, don't we?" Jo said, shouldering our satchel.

"Indeed we do," I replied. As we took up the bundles once

more, I whispered, "Miss Brocas on the throne? Surely he was speaking offhand?"

"I don't know," Jo replied grimly. "But we are about to find out."

Once we were safely in the hold we could relax a little. Those already below were too occupied to do more than give us a nod. There was a woman who seemed ill, being tended by two others; there was a man napping, and a small group counting the goods in an open crate. A quick glance told me it was foodstuffs: tea, flour, wax-sealed jars.

We piled the canvas in a corner and then Jo sat on the folded pieces, gesturing me next to her. "We should try to use the journey to rest," she said.

I took my hat off, but kept the spectacles on. They felt a kind of reassuring mask. With some wiggling and adjusting I fitted myself beside Jo and laid my head on her shoulder. She tilted her own hat low, shadowing both our faces, and tucked the satchel under her knees. It was only then that I felt just how tired I was. My few hours of sleep had been troubled by foreboding dreams—and we hadn't even arrived at Arcadia. As we dozed, I kept overhearing snatches of conversation: *we'll need a way to protect ourselves ... what harm are we doing anyone? I'm sure they will leave us alone ... but it says in the Bible ... I'll be praying for ...*

And then I heard a familiar voice say, "Where is the canvas you bought?"

At once Jo jerked upright beside me. She looked around, then quickly tugged me up and towards a crate with its lid loosely balanced on top. We opened it and bent over its contents, miming counting, as we had seen earlier.

Down the stairs came Miss Brocas with Miss Morrow close behind, their skirts whisking over the wooden steps. They toured through the hold, Miss Brocas leaning heavily on Miss Morrow's arm, discussing the yardage and oils Miss Morrow had secured. Listening to their conversation, I understood better Miss Morrow's mixed emotions with regards to Miss Brocas. They were speaking as equals: as fellow artists united in a project, with all the excitement of such. Again and again, Miss Brocas asked for Miss Morrow's experiences and shared her own. It was a conversation between like minds.

Upon reaching the canvas bundles, they spent some time feeling the weight and texture of the fabric. From their discussion I understood that Miss Morrow had been tasked with matching Miss Brocas's previous purchases to complete a series of panels.

"The man assured me there was no heavier weight to be had," Miss Morrow said. "He said with the proper sealant you could even float on it."

Miss Brocas laughed aloud at that. It was a charming laugh, girlish and high. "What a prescient fellow!" she exclaimed.

"Pardon?" Miss Morrow asked sharply.

"Wait and see, Helena, wait and see." She tucked her arm in Miss Morrow's. "Come, let us wave farewell to England."

As they walked back to the steps, Jo and I both turned to watch them. Miss Morrow, glancing back, mouthed *stay there*.

The ship creaked and groaned as the anchor was drawn up with an echoing clatter. More people descended into the hold, looking for places to sit. Some had bundles of food that they shared; two women came down with baskets full of pasties and distributed them among us. They were delicious, half savory, half sweet, their insides still warm.

"Well," Jo murmured as we nibbled our breakfast, "as threats to king and country go, this is the most kindly I have yet encountered."

"Wait and see," I replied, for my instinct told me there was a terrible abyss between these good people and Miss Brocas's laughter; an abyss in the shape of the monster and its offspring. But there was little we could do for the moment save eat and rest, the better to face what lay ahead.

It was twilight before Miss Morrow finally returned. By then there were many in the hold avoiding the chill night air. Above we could hear muffled conversations, occasionally breaking into song; down in the hold our fellow passengers whispered excitedly about their hopes for this new land. A place of freedom, they told us; a place where they could live by the sweat of their brow, without fear of crushing taxes or persecution or a dozen other violences. There were people from seemingly every walk of life, of every complexion from pitch-dark to milk-pale, all working together to make sure everyone was fed and the old and infirm were comfortable. We were told of schemes to pool labor, to create communal gardens and workshops, to bring outside trade to the island. "We five," one woman proudly declared, gesturing to a knot of women as dark-skinned as herself, "are among the best embroiderers in London. The workshops kept us in piecework, but we are going to found our own workshop on Arcadia. Soon every noblewoman in Europe will wear our handiwork."

As the conversations flowed around us, I began to truly understand what had driven so many to accept the Arcadian bargain. I had known that people throughout England suffered from a host of discriminatory practices; now I was shown, in excruciating detail, the damning picture of how my country's inequalities were inflicted upon these kind souls. Until now I had not understood the intricacies of workshops and guilds, or how brutally taxes were levied on the poorest English citizens. I had not understood the pressures, and sometimes outright violence, that white Englishpeople inflicted on their darker-skinned neighbors. Prosperous merchants threatening newcomers, designs stolen, payments withheld, valid complaints dismissed by the courts while petty crimes were given outrageous punishments ... the woes, once people began sharing, became a litany of injustices large and small. And when someone spoke of how they had considered moving to France, oh! The bitter laughter that ensued! For France was worse, they assured each other; in France it was all England's problems and more. Indeed, weren't there also French people on Arcadia? Why would they leave, if conditions were any better than England? "Well, it is *France*," one dry wit remarked, provoking more merriment.

It was amidst this laughter that Miss Morrow descended, greeting many as she made her way to us and sat beside me. I felt a rush of relief at her return, and heard Jo's audible exhale beside me.

"Penelope took a stateroom for us both; she is resting there now," she said in a low voice. "She swings from a nervous, fearful energy to laughter, often at inappropriate moments. And many here want to speak with her, yet she seems to hardly notice them."

"That doesn't seem to have lowered their spirits," Jo said.

"I'm not sure what would. So many have been desperate for any opportunity. Perhaps now you see why I felt so strongly about seeing this through?"

"We have seen many reasons to see this through," I said. "We have also seen how two artistic souls can speak to each other."

At my words Miss Morrow's eyes welled and impulsively I took her hand. "I'm sorry, I did not mean to upset you—"

"No," she gasped, "it is just that you have put your finger on the very thing. I keep thinking, what if she had never become involved in this?" Miss Morrow touched a handkerchief to her eyes, dabbing away her tears. "There were other ladies taking drawing lessons, but none sought to earn their living by it. They were simply making themselves better marriage prospects. But Penelope grew up poor, she understands what it means to, to *strive* for something. And she made Richard Loveless' reputation—! I cannot imagine working so hard only to see another's name put to my achievements. It would drive me mad; it would drive anyone mad. If we had somehow met before she married … we could have formed a workshop of our own. Our styles are highly complementary. We would have been greatly successful, I know it."

"Another life ruined by the Mastersons," Jo muttered.

"Hush! Not so loud." Miss Morrow glanced around. "Many here see Missus Masterson as their ultimate benefactor, and take their vow seriously."

The vision of our fellow passengers taking up arms made us all fall silent. Finally, Miss Morrow whispered, "Do you think they will hurt her, when they come?"

"Missus Masterson?" Jo asked.

"Penelope."

Jo and I exchanged a glance, and I nodded for Jo to speak. She had been right, in Dormouth: I had my own unproven beliefs about Miss Brocas, beliefs that might cloud my judgment.

"I hope not, Miss Morrow," Jo said. "But what Miss Brocas does next, what she chooses, may decide her fate. Anything you can do to guide her away from Missus Masterson's agenda will help tilt the scales towards mercy."

Miss Morrow nodded, but her whole body sagged at Jo's words, as if they had laid a burden on her shoulders—that her influence might be all that stood between Miss Brocas and a terrible end.

"Miss Morrow, whatever does happen? It will not be your fault," I said, squeezing her hand once more. "We will *all* do what we can to ensure Miss Brocas is treated fairly. But we, and you especially, are not responsible for her circumstances nor their outcome. We can but try—and in doing so hold responsible the woman at whose feet all this horror lies."

Again, Miss Morrow nodded. Did I see a gleam of resolve

in her eyes, did she straighten slightly? Or was I deceiving myself into seeing what I hoped was there?

"I understand," she said, then reached over and touched Jo's hand while gripping mine. "Thank you both for being here. I feel better, knowing you're close."

"Don't hesitate to raise the alarm, Miss Morrow," Jo said. "With a threat of this scale, events can become violent in an eyeblink. Trust your instincts and call at once."

"I will." She took a breath. "I will. I am going to go to her now and try to get some rest. If we cannot speak again before we reach the island? Take the canvas and ask to be directed to the studio. It's a stone outbuilding that Penelope has claimed for this project, and its location is common knowledge. That's where I will be working."

We agreed and bid Miss Morrow a good rest. Only when she was out of earshot did Jo whisper, "You and I may need to think around her."

"Oh?" I looked at her.

"She is understandably emotional about all this, and I don't think she truly grasps the scale of what might happen. I'm worried she will hesitate, thinking to protect Miss Brocas—and incur a terrible cost in doing so."

I bit my lip before I could exclaim at her words, for they were similar to my own fears, only with regards to myself. Yet already Jo was looking to me for support. I could not let her down.

"I think she is made of stronger stuff," I replied—but I could not leave it at that. The fluttering panic was rising again, as if waking from a slumber. "I too am worried," I continued, keeping my eyes on the sleeping bodies around us, choosing my words with care. "All these people, and not a one knowing of the monster. It could be a slaughter."

"Not if we have anything to say about it," Jo said firmly.

And with that I had to content myself. I settled against her to try and sleep once more … but I could not quiet the small, nagging thought, born of that brief panic: that we would not get a say, that the monster might decide everything for us, no matter our strengths or convictions.

I could not say when it was, or if indeed I was awake at all. But I found myself stirring in the night, stiff and sore from our contorted position, and saw a man looking at us from across the hold, his eyes gleaming in the darkness. I tried to awaken more fully, but when I looked again he was no longer there. A trick of my mind? Or was it the man who had shown such interest in us? I did not trust myself to wake Jo—and even as I thought this I was drifting asleep once more, as if my senses were being smothered by a heavy blanket, as if we were all under a spell.

PART II

Arcadia

CHAPTER VII

The Studio

At first Arcadia was no more than flashes of green through a dense fog that lingered despite the late morning sunlight. As everyone had crowded on deck, Jo and I decided to risk it and join them—after we had touched up our respective disguises. All were gazing raptly towards the prow as the ship penetrated the fog. For a few minutes there was only cold, grey mist, so dense it blotted out the sails above.

And then we broke through the fog, and to a one we gasped.

Arcadia gleamed like an emerald against the blue-grey water. There were a few buildings visible on its undulating surface, wisps of smoke rising from their chimneys. Sheep grazed precipitously near a sheer drop to the water below, yet the animals roamed surefooted, and I fancied I could hear their bleating. In that moment I felt as rapt, as thrilled, as everyone around us. After both our recent griefs, the prospect of a new land, free of restrictions on our persons, seemed a kind of healing. How many here were also fleeing the pain of lost relations, entailed property, pressures to conform?

Beside me Jo murmured, "It's lovely, but isolated. I heard the sailors say this fog never burns off. Let us hope Smith doesn't overshoot it."

And with that, my momentary rapture vanished, and I was once more aware of our vulnerable position. I looked behind us but there was only the fog, as opaque as a wall. Would Mr. Smith think to penetrate the fog as we had? If he overshot us, what were we to do?

My worries, however, were interrupted by more immediate concerns: the sailors were all moving, shouting instructions and racing back and forth. "What's happening?" I asked.

"Tide runs rough when you get close to shore," a voice said, making us both jump. The man from the marketplace steadied himself against the gunwale, his posture perfectly erect despite the rocking the ship. Up close, he seemed harmless enough, his grey hair a striking contrast to his tanned skin. Still, I felt a twinge of that terrible panic. Oh, why I hadn't I told Jo about him?

"It's a tricky business to enter the bay," he continued. "But they'll manage. They've done this run a few times now." He held out his hand to Jo. "I'm Stan."

"Jo Simmons, and this is my cousin Carl Read," Jo replied, clasping his hand. "Stanley—?"

"Just Stan," he said with a grin. "Let's say there's a few too many who would like to do for that other name. It will be some time before I can start giving it out again, even in Arcadia."

"I understand," Jo said feelingly.

"I bet you do. Saw you two at the market yesterday. Don't worry," he added, "I won't tell about your 'cousin.' Smart thing to do, coming to an unknown place."

The panic eased inside me as Jo smiled. "I appreciate your discretion."

"Oh, I'm discreet all right. So, what's your job to be?" At our confused expressions he clarified, "Why have you come to Arcadia? Wait, I'll guess. You're a law clerk, come to help Missus Masterson fend off claims to the island."

It was all I could do to keep my expression neutral—how close he came to Jo's actual background!—but Jo only laughed. "A little off the mark, I'm afraid. We are friends of Miss Morrow, who is working with Miss Brocas."

"Oh! The Black girl! Yes, I heard she's been hired to help in the studio. Keep it clean and such, I'm guessing." He smiled, but this time neither of us returned the expression. "Bet you can't guess what I'm here for. I'll give you a hint: it's not for my looks." He burst out laughing at his own joke.

I still couldn't bring myself to feign amusement. Something wasn't right, and it wasn't just how poorly he spoke of Miss Morrow—or was it? I no longer felt certain of my instincts.

"My guess is you're here for protection," Jo said.

At that Stan's smile became sly. "Well now. You *are* perceptive."

"Army?"

"Something like that."

"Should we be worried?" Her voice had dropped, becoming almost a murmur.

"I wish I knew." His own lips were barely moving, but his gaze was keen. "Though if I were a betting man, I would wager it's only a matter of time before someone gets curious about what she's up to."

Again, I struggled to hide my unease, for was that not our very remit here? Stan moved closer to us then. I could smell a hint of liquor on his breath, but his eyes were clear. "In fact, it's kind of surprising that she's been left alone this long. I mean, I *suppose* having someone with both English and French blood own the island is a kind of compromise … but that's assuming she doesn't do anything with it."

Jo met his gaze. "Such as populate a strategic location between the two countries with undesirables from both?"

Stan snorted. "You've put your finger upon the very thing, Mister Simmons," he said. "Perhaps you've had some military experience yourself?"

"Perhaps—" But Jo fell silent, her gaze arrested by something across the water. I turned as well, and nearly cried out in astonishment.

We had curved around the island's shore and entered a shallow bay ringed by steep, rocky hillsides topped with green grass and a hint of stone houses. The island was smaller than I had anticipated; indeed, I had seen estate grounds that rivaled it for acreage. At the northern end of the bay, however, the land rose further, forming a headland.

A headland topped by a single, vast oak tree.

I knew it at once. I knew it as well as my own house. Had I not studied its painted representation over and over, had I not dragged Mr. Morrow up that very slope, and fought for my life beneath its branches? Only now there were incongruities: where I had clambered up a steep but steady rise, part of the land had sheered away, forming a vertical drop to the beach. More striking, however, was that the oak tree itself was cleaved in two.

Jo's hand surreptitiously brushed mine and I had to fight

the urge to seize hers in turn.

"Good English oak, that," Stan opined. "Quite a few of them on the island. Missus Masterson says they're from a time when the islands were all joined together. Hopefully we won't need too many for building."

"A fine tree," Jo said, still staring. "A pity it was struck down."

Before Stan could reply the sailors began shouting again. Our pace slowed, and the boat lurched as it was buffeted by swirling currents. Sails were adjusted and dropped and the call went out to weigh anchor.

"Let's get below," Jo said in my ear, and with a touch of our hats we hurried back to the stairs. But I looked back at the tree as we descended, trying to understand. When I went through the painting, had I stepped into a past Arcadia? Or an imagined one? And what did that mean for the Leviathan? I had no answers, but it felt important that we find them— and quickly, before it was too late for us all.

My first steps upon Arcadia's shore nearly undid me. I prided myself on never swooning, but I felt decidedly dizzy as I fell into a line of people marching across the beach towards narrow wooden steps built into the hillside. I felt like we were marching to our doom. Here, Mrs. Masterson had cared for the Leviathan's eggs; there, the monster had idled, caressing its brood and responding to Mrs. Masterson's every gesture. Was it here, now, waiting beneath the waves? The thought was terrifying.

We climbed slowly, steadying each other as we struggled up the steps with our armfuls of supplies. Soon the steps absorbed all my attention, for they were steep as well as narrow, and the woman before me kept wobbling as if she were about to tumble backwards. The sun beat down upon us, drenching me in sweat. So focused was I on surviving the precarious steps that I stumbled at the summit, nearly falling against my predecessor as I had feared she would do to me.

Here, then, was Arcadia. On a flat, grassy expanse was a village of stone cottages, with more buildings in various states of repair further on. There was a small green where people were resting mid-work, there were chickens running free and sheep huddled under eaves. As we caught our breath and mopped the sweat from our faces a group of barefoot children raced across the green, shrieking with delight: the sight of their wholehearted joy made my heart lurch in my chest. I hadn't realized there would be families here, but of course there would be. Of course.

So much I hadn't thought about. I leaned against another oak tree, pretending to be overcome with heat but in truth I was trying to calm myself. Footpaths ran in several directions, disappearing over softly undulating rises. I glimpsed a plowed field in the distance. All in all, it could have been any village, anywhere. How had both governments ignored Arcadia for so long? Unless fog and tide together had kept it forgotten?

Jo asked a passing fellow the way to the studio and he pointed us down a path that wound away from the green. A long building, he said, to the left of the castle. Perhaps there was a ruin on the island? There was a great deal of clamor now, as more boatloads of people arrived. A table set up before one of the cottages seemed to be distributing papers, and a large map of the island was being passed around, showing rectangular plots of land. All in all, it felt quite organized, with a veneer of authority—except, of course, the only authority here was Mrs. Masterson.

We set out for the studio, weaving around the knots of waiting people—

And just then came a distant cacophony of screams.

Everyone stopped where they were, astounded. A few women screamed as if in echo. Jo and I both dropped our canvas bundles in shock, my stomach vanishing sickeningly, Jo reaching under her coat for the pistol. The sound of the women's cries underscored what I already knew: the initial screams had not been human. They were thin, higher-pitched versions of the sound that sometimes haunted my dreams.

"Everyone, it is all right." One of the men distributing papers stood up; his English was accented, and he repeated the words in a fluent French. "Madame Masterson keeps a menagerie in the castle," he explained, pitching his voice so it would carry. "In fact, we are to see it tomorrow, for after the morning service there will be a festival to welcome all of you to Arcadia, and Madame has promised to show us her creatures."

Cheers went up as he repeated the information in French, but they seemed to come from a distance. My breath was suddenly loud in my ears, my heart racing; everything around me wobbled until I thought I might faint. Over and over the thoughts drummed in my mind: the eggs had hatched, they had hatched *here*, now, and whatever she was plotting it would happen *tomorrow* …

And Mr. Smith wouldn't come until the day after, if indeed he came at all.

I looked at Jo. My fear must have shown in my face for she grasped my arm. "It changes nothing," she whispered. "Caro! It changes nothing. We must get to Miss Morrow now."

"They hatched." My voice was trembling. "Oh Jo, they *hatched* …"

"And yet they're small enough to be kept at this castle. Caro, *think*. You saw those eggs just weeks ago. How large could they have grown since then? And we don't know how many survived. It may be just one or two, all no larger than a good-sized fish."

It took all my resolve to shove my rising panic down. All she said was plausible, and if we faced several creatures the size of the Leviathan we would have known by now, for how could Mrs. Masterson keep such monsters hidden? Or so I told myself over and over, trying to smother my fearful thoughts, my hand drifting upwards to rest gently on my sternum.

Breathe, that's my girl.

It seemed an age before I could make myself nod, though I knew it had been but a moment. Certainly, Jo seemed to think I was better, for she handed me my canvas bundle and took up her own and our satchel. "Let's focus on Miss Morrow," she said encouragingly.

We set out again for the studio. At least with such a crowd it was easy to pass unnoticed. There was no sign of Miss Morrow or Miss Brocas, or Stan for that matter. The path dipped and rose, passing by a large vegetable patch ringed with blooming flowers. We passed two brown-skinned women leading a pig, who smiled and nodded at us, and we inclined our heads in turn—only to jump in fright as the unearthly screaming rose up again. "Those damned birds!" one of the women exclaimed, only to be admonished for her language by the other woman, and we all laughed a little too loudly. After them we passed a tall, gangly redheaded man with a tool bag who was bellowing for his teenaged relation to keep up, they were supposed to have started work that morning. The boy was carrying a sack of what looked like shingles, sweating profusely under their weight. Past the vegetable garden was a crumbling stone hut being rebuilt, a man and woman just visible inside as they worked to hang a new front door. It was all charmingly bucolic—or it would have been, save for those dread cries—but it also spoke to me of many months of residence. *A couple years*, they had said in the dinghy. All to create a tiny nation here in the middle of the Channel—one that included former soldiers in its populace.

The path wound down into a hollow, as if we were descending into the navel of the island. Here the oak trees were older, grander; here too there were fruit trees, trailing vines, a brightness of color that made me think of my father's books about southern expeditions. It was so vivid it felt almost painful to look at. I desperately wanted to pull my hat lower, but my arms were full of canvas.

"Bloody hell, it's bright out today," Jo said.

"Language," I murmured. "But it's surprising, isn't it? It feels almost tropical, or what I imagine tropical to be."

"It feels downright strange. Doesn't it feel strange?"

I hesitated, but I too felt unnerved. "Yes. It's too bright, too hot. And there are birds, I've seen them flying, but no birdsong. I wonder if the others have noticed?"

"Unless they think it's related to her so-called menagerie?" Jo sighed. "So many of these people are fleeing dire circumstances, it's no wonder they're quick to explain things away. I'm sure they will have a similar story for the lack of birdsong, or the weather … It's that fog that has me really worried. If it never burns off, a ship sitting outside it won't be able to see our signal, and a ship inside will be visible to everyone on the island. And I suspect Stan isn't the first soldier she's recruited. They may already have plans to deal with intruders."

"You think if Mister Smith tries to annex the island, he will be sailing into an ambush?"

"I think there are several possibilities and I don't like any of them."

We had reached a fork in the path. To our right, it curved towards a copse of trees through which we could just glimpse a curtain wall and tower, but this was no picturesque ruin. The wall and tower, at least, were perfectly intact. To our left, the path ran to a long stone outbuilding with a newly-thatched roof, perhaps once a stable. Behind it, a field of grass rippled gently in the breeze.

"That must be the studio," Jo said, and struck out for the building. I followed, though my eyes kept straying to the castle. A Norman edifice, all sharp angles and grey stone, with a thin trail of smoke rising from beyond the wall. Was this how Mrs. Masterson envisioned herself, a queen over this small domain?

As we drew close I saw that the studio had indeed been a stable once. The stall openings were covered with heavy oak boards save for two that seemed to function as doorways. Jo cautiously said, "Hullo?" but there was no response. She moved ahead of me and stepped inside, then waved me in after her.

Inside, the stalls had been removed, creating a large, open space. We placed our bundles in a corner and began exploring. In the center of the far wall was another broad opening, its gates swung outwards to reveal a paddock beyond. There leaning against a wall were large, round wooden frames with holes drilled into them that seemed oddly familiar—and then I placed it: they resembled embroidery hoops, only taller than a man. Perhaps they were to stretch the canvas to keep it taut for painting.

If Miss Brocas had enough panels, and stitched them together, could she make a painting large enough for the Leviathan to pass through? But that seemed the work of weeks, perhaps months …

Jo was at the far end of the room, studying a table. "Caro," she murmured.

I hurried to her side. Several sketches had been laid out, with rocks holding the corners down. Not preliminary sketches as I knew them: these seemed more like diagrams. They showed small circles linked together, like beads in a necklace. Each had a strange symbol drawn in the middle.

"This one looks familiar," I said, tapping a symbol. "I swear I saw something like it on a barn door back home, only I cannot remember where."

"There was a cunning woman that my mother used to visit

when we were sick," Jo said. "My father hated when she went there, said it was peasant nonsense. But this was carved in the doorframe of her house." She traced another of the shapes with a finger. "Old beliefs."

"What's in the center?" For there was a kind of wavy, swirling stippling between the circles, filling the space.

"I don't know, but it must mean something." She shook her head, looking around. "We best see what else we can discover. There's no telling when they will come down here."

Beside the sketches there was a jar with an array of large brushes: not the delicate tools of Miss Morrow's studio, but the kind used to paint houses. There were clean smocks hanging on pegs and lidded buckets of water. Behind a door at one narrow end I found a smaller room with a made-up cot and a washbasin atop a stool. Clearly someone was expected to sleep here. In the room was a window and another door leading to the field. With a glance back at Jo I went out to explore.

The sun was gloriously warm and insects buzzed over the waving grass. In better circumstances it would be a pleasant place to live and work. Although I could not see the castle over the roof, I sensed its presence. Were Miss Morrow to aid Miss Brocas, she would be doing so under Mrs. Masteron's watchful eye, and a stone's throw from the source of that horrible screeching.

Against the wall of the studio were two fat barrels, waist-high and rounded. I was reminded of the one I had hidden inside at Medby … but now was not the time for such fearful reminisces. I nudged the nearer one and found it full. As its contents sloshed, a sickly aroma rose up and my heart began to race once more.

"Jo," I called.

She was outside at once, her hand under her sleeve where her knife rested. "What—oh," she said, sniffing. "Oh God."

"If we open one, they'll know—"

"If we don't, we won't know for certain."

I hesitated but for a moment and then I drew out my own knife. Together we prised up one of the lids.

And then we both stepped back, gagging. It was the same rotting flesh I had smelled in Miss Brocas's studio, but instead of a putrefying slime, this was a smooth liquid, viscous and opaque. Holding a handkerchief over her face, Jo picked up a twig and swirled it inside, then held it up. The liquid barely dripped. Like honey, though it was the furthest thing from.

"Well," she said, her voice muffled by the cloth, "at least we know for certain they're trying again."

"If they blend it with pigments, or treat the canvas in some way? There is enough there to cover many, many paintings."

"Or one vast one?"

"But the work involved—! I cannot but think it would take weeks. Yet Miss Morrow said she was brought here to *finish* a commission—"

I broke off as we both heard it: a distant rumbling, drawing closer, the mingled sounds of cart wheels and several voices conversing. Swiftly we pressed the lid back into place, though we did not dare beat upon it lest we were heard. Then Jo dragged me around the side of the studio and into the denser brush across the path. We had just dropped into the shrubbery when Miss Brocas, Miss Morrow, and a half-dozen men and women came over the rise, the latter steering two carts loaded with barrels from the ship.

Bringing up the rear, a rifle slung over his shoulder, was Stan, flanked by two other fellows, including the one who had been walking with him in Dormouth.

As they reached the studio, the screaming cries rose up yet again. At least two such voices, I could hear now, the latter trailing off into a gurgle. Everyone jumped, Miss Morrow most of all; when Miss Brocas reached for her, she hurried ahead into the studio. Stan directed the two men to opposite ends of the path. The others began maneuvering the barrels off the carts, glancing nervously at the castle walls as they worked. Stan positioned himself near them.

In the center of the path, Miss Brocas stopped and raised her head. The sun fell on her ghastly, pale face, revealing watery eyes sunk into purpled sockets. I realized then that as much as I feared what Mr. Smith's forces would do to her, she might not survive that long. Whatever this task was, it was killing her, as surely as any sickness.

She nodded at the sky. I twisted a little, looking over my shoulder. Through the overhanging trees I saw the castle wall. Atop another tower stood a figure in a similar white dress, her long grey hair gently stirring in the breeze: Mrs. Masterson, alive, present, watching us all.

We lay in the brush for what seemed like an age. Stan paced leisurely, now and again making eye contact with each of his seconds in some silent exchange. If their presence was strange to the others—for why should anyone bear arms in a united community, or guard a common path?—they made no sign, but swiftly unloaded the carts and began pulling them back towards the village. Besides the barrels, they had also brought two hampers of food and several corked bottles. Clearly Miss Brocas and Miss Morrow were to spend some time here while they worked on the "commission."

"Stan's lads are sticking around," Jo said in my ear. "What exactly are they guarding?"

Suddenly Miss Morrow appeared, holding a kerchief over her face, and began retching into the grass beside the studio. Jo exhaled beside me and I nodded; we knew what she had just discovered. Stan hurried to her side but before he could address her, Miss Brocas spoke sharply to him and he stepped back as she took Miss Morrow forcibly by the arm and steered her down the path—closer to us. With a gesture, she sent the guard back to Stan so they could speak in private. I strained to hear their conversation, but all I could hear was Miss Morrow's high, sharp tone and Miss Brocas pleading. As they spoke, the screaming cries came again and Miss Morrow gestured at the castle, punctuating her words with jabs of her finger while Miss Brocas shook her head. At last, Miss Brocas began weeping and flung her arms around Miss Morrow's neck. Miss Morrow took a deep breath, then slowly patted Miss Brocas on the back, as one would do to a child.

"Real, or a ploy?" Jo whispered, and I nodded again, for I had the same concern. As genuine as her sorrow appeared, Miss Brocas was as capable of deceit as anyone, and Miss Morrow too earnest and good-hearted to not give her the benefit of doubt.

They went into the studio, but I saw now that Stan was frowning. One of his fellows spoke in his ear, his expression equally disturbed, and Stan nodded. He looked up at the castle, then walked around to the back of the studio. When he reemerged, his expression was even more grim, but it became placid the moment Miss Brocas came out. She and Stan walked up the path together, followed by Stan's seconds.

"Now," Jo said as soon as they vanished over the rise, but I laid a hand on her arm, twisting once more to see the tower behind us.

The figure of Mrs. Masterson was gone.

"Missus Masterson was watching," I whispered at Jo's raised eyebrow.

"Wonderful," Jo muttered. "Still, we must risk it."

We darted across to the far end of the studio, where the little anteroom was. As soon as we were in the shadow of the wall, we looked back at the castle again. There was still no figure atop the tower, but who might be watching from its narrow, dark windows?

"Miss Morrow," I called softly, tapping the window. "Miss Morrow, are you there?"

At once she appeared, her brown face visibly grayer, and swung open the casement. "Thank goodness," she gasped. "Have you heard them? She claims it's birds, hah! I know what exotic birds sound like, I've drawn plenty in my time. And you will not believe—there is this, this *slime* in the back—"

"We saw," Jo interrupted. "Is Miss Brocas returning?"

"Yes, she has just gone to oversee the last two carts, she'll return with them."

"And Stan?"

"He's apparently to watch over her. Him or one of his men, at all times. To see to anything she might need, he claims. You must take care, they are all armed."

"Are you all right?" I asked.

Miss Morrow took a breath. "It has been a shock, all of it. First the armed guards, then those dreadful noises, and then the barrels … I know you warned me, but to see it—to *smell* it …" She took another breath. "She swore to me it's a kind of sealant, which I know to be another lie. But she then begged me not to leave her, she will go mad without me …"

"Miss Morrow. *Helena*," Jo said forcefully, getting her attention. "Don't think of her words, don't think of the Arcadians. Look in your heart and tell us: do you want to leave?"

"I'm all right, truly."

"That's not what I am asking. You have played your role. You brought us here. We can find you a hiding place, perhaps even get you to Mister Smith's ship. Do you want to leave?"

Miss Morrow fell silent, but at last she shook her head. "Not yet. I still do not understand what she's plotting. She is creating circles of canvas to float atop the water—as an ornament for the festival, she says. A way of honoring the fishermen here. She claims other displays are being built for farmers and craftspeople, but I have seen no evidence of such. Clearly there is an evil purpose at work, and unless we understand the exact mechanism, we won't know how to stop it."

"Unless we simply signal Mister Smith now," Jo said, "and he annexes Arcadia before Missus Masterson can act."

"And what of the people? They're just trying to make better lives for themselves! They have committed no crimes. Would you drag them back to even greater misery, now that they spent their last pennies getting here?" Her voice grew stronger as she spoke. "If we can figure out what she's planning, we can sabotage it at a moment's notice—and if we let her scheme proceed, armed with that precaution, the people themselves might rise up against her. We could end this without the violence of annexation."

"That is a lot of ifs, Miss Morrow," I said gently.

"Do you have a better plan, then?" She looked at me, her eyebrows arched, and for a moment I thought I was looking at her brother, so firm was her resolve.

"Not yet," Jo said. "But we also haven't had any breakfast. Will you be here tonight?"

"I believe so. Penelope asked for a second bed, but she also spoke of dining with Missus Masterson and spending the night in the castle. I pleaded work, and that was no lie: if she wants this done by morning it will take much of the night." She shuddered as she glanced in the direction of the castle. "Are those noises the monster, then?"

"The castle is not big enough to house the Leviathan," I said. At her alarmed look I managed to smile, though I suspected my expression was more ghastly than reassuring. "We think that sound is its young, being kept nearby."

For a moment Miss Morrow looked truly frightened—I could almost see her measuring the castle in her mind—and then she shook herself. "Stan said this island used to be a smuggler's haven. Perhaps there's an inlet or a cove on the far side of the castle?"

"We can look for such while we scout the coastline," Jo said, looking at me. "We need to try to get above the fog to signal the ship—and think of what to do if we cannot. We will come back to you after sundown and report our findings. Caro, what do you think?"

I nodded. "The more information we have to hand, the better. There is too much unknown here, both in Arcadia and the temperament of the people. They may well be ignorant of Missus Masterson's intent, but it's also possible that some support her. This family has persuaded sensible folk before."

We fell silent for a moment, each thinking of the many victims in this—and I suspect Miss Morrow's thoughts went to Miss Brocas. "Agreed," she said. "If you cut across the field, I believe there's a second, smaller path that leads back to the village." As we rose, she added suddenly, "Take care, please, both of you?" Her smile was strained. "Without you I shall be quite bereft, and Frannie always said if I died doing something foolish he would plant asters on my grave. I hate asters, they make me sneeze horribly."

At that Jo laughed, and I squeezed Miss Morrow's hand through the window. "We'll see you tonight," I reassured her. I only hoped events would not make me a liar.

CHAPTER VIII

An Ally Returns

We crossed the field as Miss Morrow had suggested and headed back to the village. Halfway there we paused to touch up our disguises again, and I had to laugh: we were both disheveled, sweaty, and lightheaded from lack of sustenance. "I'm not sure we are meant for this," I said as I dabbed makeup on Jo's face. "I suspect proper spies remember to bring food and drink at least."

Jo laughed. "Yes, and that goes double for me, having been at this longer. But as a perceptive and lovely lady has often told me, I can be a poor planner at the best of times."

I blushed at the *lovely*. "Well, before we walk all over this island, perhaps we should try to keep from fainting? There must be a way to get food—"

I paused as we heard something: a faint rustling, not quite the wind. "Stan may have sent someone back," Jo said, her lips barely moving.

I looked down, so my hat shielded my face. "Do we change plans?"

"We are still two friends of Miss Morrow, in search of a meal." She quickly packed the satchel again. "But I think it best to keep our voices low."

We began walking once more. I kept looking around, but there was nothing, not a hint of another presence, still I now felt eyes upon me—or did I? Oh, that I could feel more certain in myself!

"I feel as if we are investigating three Arcadias," Jo murmured. "This fledgling community, the strange circles at the studio, and whatever is making those noises."

"Four," I corrected. "The community, the circles and their purpose, the so-called menagerie, and the Arcadia in the painting."

"I wonder what Stan thinks he's protecting. We should look more closely at that tree. How long ago was the damage? There may have been a recent storm. And it looked to be one of the highest points on the island; we may be able to signal from there."

I nodded, but I knew the damage wasn't recent. I had weathered many storms in my childhood, being so close to the coast. The distance had been great, but I had seen none of the bright, raw wood of a recent lightning strike. Inwardly I was convinced that the scarring was old, very old. That somehow the tree in the paintings was from a different *time*, and that was where Mrs. Masterson had hidden the Leviathan. How had it gotten there, how she might bring it back?

What if she had already brought it back?

But there were dozens of people on Arcadia now, including fishermen. Someone would have noticed a massive creature in the water. And there was the matter of feeding it—it and its offspring. How was she keeping them alive?

With these musings, we reached the outer edge of the

village. Now that we were less burdened, we took our time perusing the few storefronts. There was a blacksmith at the far end of the street, with an ironmonger's wares on a table in front. There was what appeared to be a chandlery, where two young men were unpacking some of the crates from our ship. In front of a cottage beside the chandlery, the embroidery women were busily sorting bolts of cloth and sewing supplies, perhaps setting up as mercers while they started their export scheme. A small building bore the old-fashioned pole of a barber-surgeon, with a note tacked to the door: *Back at dinnertime*. Behind where the check-in table had stood was a last, large building, now smelling wonderfully of hot food. Approaching from inland, we saw there were a few tables and benches beside it. One of the tables was occupied by a large party, all dressed in rough clothes with bits of grass and leaves still clinging to them, enjoying two pies between them and several tankards.

"Tavern," Jo said delightedly. "God be praised."

"We're getting looks," I murmured, for indeed several people were openly staring at us, with less than welcoming expressions. Or was it simply my own unease, discoloring my perceptions? Stan's seconds, at least, were nowhere among them.

"Everyone from our ship is probably getting looked at. We're new, after all," Jo soothed me. "But I will ask if we can take our food under that tree there, out of the sun. We'll be tucked away nicely."

As she spoke my stomach growled. Our last meal had been the pasty on the ship, and the pie smelled wonderful. We ducked inside the building, nearly tripping over a man repairing a window frame. The floor beneath our feet was freshly laid, the bar before us newly fitted and gleaming with varnish. The kitchen beyond was clearly bustling. The woman behind the bar had her back to us as she stacked clean plates and when Jo cleared her throat, she turned around.

We found ourselves gaping at Madame Viart.

But this was not the elegant procuress we had met in Medby. This woman was as apple-cheeked as a farmer's wife, her black hair braided and pinned up. Her eyes were the same sparkling blue, her figure enviable even in her plain linen dress and apron, but she could have been any barmaid, anywhere. For a moment she frowned at our expressions, and then comprehension dawned over her features. She made a little cutting gesture and leaned over the bar. "What can I get for you?" she asked. Her familiar voice, with its accented English, made me cringe in memory. *An unwritten promissory note, from you to me.*

"We are in desperate need of food," Jo said.

"You are off the last ship, then?" Her eyes gleamed as she spoke, and when Jo nodded, she continued, "We currently have two forms of payment. You can pay in your king's coin, or you can pay in work. Today we are asking that you clean your dishes and unpack and store one crate of goods." She paused, then added significantly, "I can show you the unpacking after you eat, it's very easy."

"Then we choose easy, and to keep our coin," Jo replied with a smile.

"Very well. Pie or sausages with new potatoes, which would you prefer?"

Jo looked at me and I mouthed *pie*. "Two slices of pie, if you please, and whatever you have to drink."

With a brisk nod, Madame Viart disappeared into the back, swiftly returning with two generous wedges of pie on pewter plates. She laid them on the bar with utensils and, taking up two tankards, moved to a cask with a spigot.

"Are you from France, then?" Jo asked.

Madame Viart gave her a slit-eyed look over her shoulder, and oh! That was the woman we knew, for better or worse. "I am from Brittany," she declared. "I am, in a way, as English as you."

"When did you come to Arcadia?"

"Some weeks ago." She placed the first tankard before us, then began pulling the second. Again, she gave us a slit-eyed look, then jerked her head towards the far wall of the tavern. But there was nothing there save some tools and scraps of wood, and a large, framed print, a map of some kind.

With a glance at Jo, I moved closer, only to find myself struggling to understand what I was seeing. At first it seemed the outline of some foreign land, until I saw the neatly-printed words within the land mass: *London, Paris.*

Between them, larger than both, was a third name: *Arcadia.*

What I was looking at was a map of our part of Europe, but with the Channel reduced to an inlet and England and France completely joined—and this little island now a capital city. But how? When? Or was it just a fantastical image, the product of some fevered mind?

Jo came up behind me, the satchel wedged high on her shoulder so she could balance our plates on one crooked arm, while clutching our tankards in her other hand. Quickly I divested her of our plates as she studied the map. "What on earth is this?" she whispered.

"I don't know," I whispered back. "But the placement of the cities looks accurate, doesn't it?"

"Yes ... but the whole image is impossible. Perhaps a kind of fantastic geography?" Jo nudged me. "We can eat under the tree. She says when we're finished, she will show us where to wash our things."

Outside we settled in the tree's dense shade. The first mouthful of pie made me nearly dizzy with pleasure and it took much to keep myself from wolfing it down. "I wonder if she has some way of getting information off the island," Jo continued, her lips barely moving.

I swallowed down a large mouthful. "Even if she does, is there time to use it? The festival is tomorrow, and we still need to get back to Miss Morrow."

"We should bring her with us. She's been here for weeks; we shouldn't plan anything without knowing what she knows."

"A sensible proposal, save for one possible complication." At Jo's confused look I explained, "Does Miss Morrow know of her, and does she know of Miss Morrow?"

"What—*oh*," Jo breathed. "Yes, I hadn't thought of that."

We knew from our previous acquaintance that Miss Morrow had been upset by her brother traveling overseas, without word to his family; we also knew that he had spent at least some of that time in Madame Viart's intimate company. How much had Mr. Morrow told his sister? How would Miss Morrow feel about conspiring with her brother's mistress?

Finally Jo murmured, "Cross that bridge when we come

to it," and went back to eating her pie. But the taste was less delightful than when we had first sat down, and we ate mechanically, each contemplating what lay before us.

We washed our dishes in the kitchen under the watchful eye of Madame Viart, the cook, a boy chopping vegetables, and a girl whose one job seemed to be stirring a large pot without cease. All three welcomed us to Arcadia and thanked us for helping out. "If you're looking for work, don't hesitate to ask," the cook said over his shoulder.

Afterwards Madame Viart took us into a narrow, cool pantry with several crates stacked haphazardly. We opened one and began shelving packets of tea. Madame Viart peeked back through the doorway, then said in a low voice, "We must be careful. Many here visit with that woman."

I thought of the white-clad figure atop the tower and shuddered. "What is the meaning of the map?" I whispered, while at the same time Jo asked, "Do you know what she intends?"

"She came some days ago and said we were to hang the map, something about how it is our destiny, she wants us all to see it," Madame Viart replied with a shrug. "They humor her because she gives them land for free, and then behind her back they worry she's getting old." She tapped her forehead. "You know of the fête tomorrow? I heard a few of the others saying she wants sacrifices, only they think she means chickens, or perhaps a sheep." Another slit-eyed look, this one in the direction of the cook. "That one thinks it's a funny peasant thing. 'My grandmama killed rabbits for the forest spirits, she threw fish back in the rivers, it's just old ladies and their foolishness.'"

I looked at Jo, alarmed, but before we could confer, Madame Viart grabbed my arm. "I want off this damn island. Stanley suspects me, I know it. I want to see Francis! You must take me to him."

The blue eyes were welling, the rosy cheeks deepening in color. Jo, however, simply said, "Hush. He's not here and he's not coming. You will have to make do with us. Can you—"

"Not coming?" She looked from myself to Jo and back. "You're lying! He promised he would join me here, he's never broken his word."

"He was injured, Madame," I said as calmly as I could, but my words still elicited a squawk of fright. "He will recover completely, I promise," I added hurriedly before she could speak. "Only he's not yet strong enough to travel."

"Then *you* must get me out of here," she retorted. "You owe me—"

Before she could complete the dreaded phrase, Jo hissed us into silence while she peeked outside the pantry. My stomach was knotting—if Madame Viart called in that debt now—oh why hadn't I told Jo before this?

"Just that kitchen lad," Jo said. "Now look, Madame. We will all get out of here *if* we work together. Can you get a message out?"

"I send my messages back on the ships, only this one won't sail until Monday." She made a little sobbing noise. "My poor Francis! Though perhaps it's for the best … my beauty is already ruined, no one even has hair oil here. Animals! He will never love me again ..."

At that moment the terrible screaming came once more. Madame Viart gave a cry and fell against me. "Those monsters!" she gasped. "And they think it's birds! We're all going to die ..."

"Ellie!" The cook called. "Ellie, there's custom."

"Those beasts made me spill the tea," she called back.

"Well, hurry up. I'll send Susie but I don't want that gravy to burn."

"Madame, *please* pay attention," Jo said. "We are meeting tonight to discuss what to do—including possibly leaving. Could you meet us after sundown?"

"I have to work supper," she said miserably. "Perhaps afterwards ... but if you cannot get me away ..."

"Only we desperately need your help," Jo continued. "Helena Morrow is here as well, she is in the studio by the castle. Brought here by *that woman*."

The transformation was nothing short of astonishing. For a heartbeat, Madame Viart openly gaped at Jo, and then all her misery vanished and she once more became the haughty madame from Medby, her chin raised, new resolve in her features. "Francis's sister? The little hellion?"

Jo nodded solemnly. "She lacks our ... experience, Madame, but she has all her brother's courage and stubbornness. Any action we consider must include her welfare."

"Yes," she said. "Yes, of course." Her blue eyes became unfocused as she thought. "Does she—does she know of me?"

"We don't know," I said. "Madame, please come tonight—"

Footsteps outside caused us all to snatch up the last of the tea just as the cook stuck his head in the pantry. "Ellie! How long does it take to unpack one bleeding crate? I've got four out here now and the gravy burning."

"Coming," Madame Viart said. At the doorway, however, she mouthed *after sundown* and Jo mouthed *the studio,* and with a single nod she was gone.

And with that we had to content ourselves.

With our bellies and minds full, we struck out for the headland with the dead oak. Although the sun beat down from a cloudless sky, we could see the grey wall of fog just off the coastline, so solid it erased the horizon. As we started climbing up the rise, we saw that the fog encircled the island completely. A passing ship might think it merely unusual weather; only from within the circle could one see how precise it was.

"How can that fog be natural?" I asked, pausing halfway up. "I've never seen anything like it."

"It looks like it was painted there," Jo replied. When I looked at her, startled, she shrugged. "It was the first thing that came to mind."

"If Missus Masterson is capable of such, such *magic*—"

"That is a very great if," she said soothingly. "Were you not just advising Miss Morrow about *if*s? We will all do better to stay focused on the *w*s: what, when, why."

I nodded, but her words did little to soothe my unease. If Mrs. Masterson was capable of manipulating the very weather, all the *w*s might be moot. But perhaps Madame Viart could shed light on that as well.

The ascent was as steep as I remembered, and between the strain of the climb, my fearful memories, and the beating sun, I felt decidedly queasy when we finally reached the top. What met us there, however, was no if: the oak tree had indeed been struck long ago. That we recognized it at all was testament to its vigor at the time of the blast. What remained now looked almost petrified.

"We both saw it," Jo said. "It was green, it was alive, mere weeks ago." She craned her head around. "Perhaps we made a mistake?"

"The beach is the same," I said, peering over the edge. "It was a gentler slope down, but I remember those rocks jutting out. The hill ran down to the edge of the sand, about where those birds are …" I trailed off, sickened by the memory: of the vast beast looming over the beach, its tentacles waving in uncanny mimicry of Mrs. Masterson's gestures. Quickly I looked back at the island, thinking to soothe myself with its green vistas—

Only to see a flash of movement at the base of the hill. I strained to see, tilting my hat to shield against the sun: nothing.

Jo was shaking her head at the fog. "We don't stand a chance at signaling if it stays that dense."

Still, I squinted at the path below. A trick of the light? "They won't see our signal, but one of the Arcadians might."

"An excellent point," she said with a sigh. "Which is also the flaw in my second plan: if we try to row out in a dinghy, we'll be visible from half the island. Even at night it will be chancey."

I tore my eyes away from the path and looked at the water

once more, watching the strangely silent birds wheeling over the beach below. At every turn we might be seen, and if we were being followed already …

And then it struck me. "If we cannot sail past the fog, we should look for a cannon," I said.

"A *cannon*?" Jo laughed. "What does my country girl know of cannons?"

"I know that castles often have them, and smugglers like them very much." I grinned at her then. "We do have smugglers up north, you know."

"And the sound will carry in all directions. Darling, you are brilliant."

"I learned from the best," I replied, my grin broadening at her blush. For the first time I could see it: a way out of this mess, with just a single spark.

"Did anyone ever tell you, Caroline Daniels, that you are exquisitely lovely when contemplating gunplay?" Jo asked throatily.

Her hand had wiggled under my coat, teasing the sweat-damp fabric beneath. I turned to her completely, and saw it again: just a hint of movement in the trees below us.

"I think we should keep moving," I said softly. And Jo, to her credit, didn't press me for an explanation. She merely shouldered the satchel and began marching through the heat once more.

It was late in the afternoon when we finally rounded the southern end of the island and came in sight of the castle.

In truth, Arcadia was a lovely place. In better circumstances I would have liked to visit properly, get to know the people better; perhaps—

—just perhaps, if it could become all that it hoped to be—

—we might even have considered settling here, at least for a while. To see if *hope* could become *home*.

But these were not better circumstances.

Behind us the path dipped and rose, dipped and rose. We had seen no further movement, but we made a good show of playing the newly arrived nonetheless, striding up to every headland and pointing and exclaiming, though in truth they were exclamations of dismay. Every possible place to sail from, or for rescue to put ashore, was marked by violently crashing waves. The only placid surf was the bay—in full view of the village, and most likely the site of tomorrow's festival.

Now the castle's ramparts came into view in the hollow below us, though our vantage was not high enough to let us see into the bailey. Beside it we could just make out the long roof of the studio between the trees. As we watched, Miss Morrow and Miss Brocas emerged, carrying a hoop between them. A piece of canvas had been stretched over it, with one of the symbols painted in its center; its whole surface glistened in the reddening sunlight. They laid it carefully in the field beside a second hoop, weighing down the edges, and went back into the studio.

"I wonder if she's figured out a way to undermine the paintings," I said.

"Possibly a moot concern," Jo replied. "Look at that far turret on the castle, the one closest to the water—and there!

On the wall as well, between the turrets."

I followed her gaze and nearly clapped my hands like a child, as much from relief as delight. "Oh, Jo. Could it really be that simple?"

Up against the crenellated wall that topped the turret like a crown was a long, dark shape, with a pyramid of spheres beside it: a cannon and shot. Three similar shapes were placed strategically along the ramparts, all pointed at the sea.

"Simple, I doubt. But definitely possible. And our best chance at sending a clear signal." She bit her lip. "We need a way in. And I don't mean Miss Morrow, before you make the suggestion."

"I wasn't going to suggest her," I admonished. "Perhaps Madame Viart can help? She works at the tavern, and even the likes of Missus Masterson must eat." I frowned. "At least, I'm assuming she eats."

"Well. This is going to be quite a night." Jo looked over the castle again. "Oh Caro," she whispered, "if we can pull this off …"

"We will," I said, and then softer, "we will." Perhaps if I said it enough, I could make myself believe it.

And it seemed to work. Jo's expression became one of fixed resolve, a set of her features I knew all too well. "All right," she said. "Let's do this."

CHAPTER IX

Plots and Counterplots

We waited until sundown before approaching the studio. As the sky tinged red, we saw Miss Brocas leave and head for the castle. Only then did we move forward, Jo striking out left and I going right, in case Stan had left men watching and one of us was spotted. I found myself crawling through underbrush, pausing every few minutes to check for movement and to place Jo. What if she was taken? The thought brought back my sickening fear and I quickly tamped it down. Only when I glimpsed her hat, at the far side of the pasture, did I dart in a crouch towards the back of the studio. The paddock gates had been closed, but a lantern gleamed in the anteroom's window. Past the roof I could see torches flickering on the castle wall like stars. I kept in the deep shadows as I aimed for the anteroom's door. When a hissing noise rose up from the brush across the path I nearly cried out.

"It is I," whispered Madame Viart, wiggling out from behind a shrub. She hissed again as twigs pulled at her skirts, then hurried over to crouch against the wall beside me.

"Hush! You'll bring them down upon us," I whispered. "Were you followed?"

She sniffed. "Certainly not! I know my business."

"Good. Have you seen Jo? She was coming from the far side of the field."

"I want to talk to you," Madame Viart whispered, as if I hadn't spoken. "Alone."

"For God's sake. We need to get inside—"

"You made me a promise," she hissed.

My heart sank at her words. "Yes," I agreed, and with a glance around, I drew her back towards the gates. Madame Viart followed, an ungainly crab with her skirts sprawling around her knees. What if Jo came upon us now? Oh, I should have told her before this, why hadn't I told her?

Because I had feared her anger. Because I hadn't wanted to hear her say, *you shouldn't have done it. You should have found another way or let me go.* Because I had feared losing our fledgling bond. It all seemed so foolish now—but what then of my panic in Dormouth?

"Madame, please," I whispered once she was beside me again. "We cannot get off the island right now—"

"No, no," she interrupted. "You must make her like me."

"Pardon?" I stared at her.

"Francis's sister. Helena. Make her like me. Tell her I am a good woman of fine character."

For a moment I could only gape at her. "Madame, you were Thomas Masterson's mistress," I finally managed. "*And* you were running a brothel. Not exactly a respectable profession."

"At the order of the king!" she replied, outraged. "Otherwise, I would have never done such things. Thomas was so, so *pointy, and* he smelled like cabbage. Do you know, in bed—"

"Yes, yes, I'm sure it was terrible," I put in hurriedly. "But

I cannot simply *make* her like you. She will judge for herself, no matter what I say."

"But you can explain that I love Francis," she gasped. "That I want to marry him, properly marry him."

Again I stared, now truly astonished. "You want to marry Francis Morrow," I repeated.

"He won't propose, no matter how I hint," she whispered. "But if his sister likes me—for him the sun rises and sets on her—oh, what if he dies and I haven't told him I love him? What if she dies?" Her eyes were welling. "What if we all die?"

And then she flung her arms around me and began to weep.

"My God," Jo whispered from the darkness. "We'll bring the whole island down on us. What is going on?"

"You wouldn't believe me if I told you," I whispered back, though I felt a rush of relief as she drew near. Still, Madame Viart wept as I patted her back awkwardly. "Mister Morrow will recover," I whispered. "Our task right now is to make sure we all live to see him again."

"I told him he shouldn't leave Paris," she wept into my coat. "I told him the English are animals, all of them. When I find who hurt him, I will kill them with my bare hands."

"Yes. Well." I patted her back again. "Ah, shall we go inside? Miss Morrow will be dreadfully worried."

But that only brought fresh complaint, for now she looked frightful and Miss Morrow would think her hideous. Jo, unable to restrain herself any longer, reached over, forced Madame Viart's head up, and wiped roughly at her face with a handkerchief. I thought she was making matters worse, but after a moment Madame Viart snatched the handkerchief away with a glower and proceeded to dab at her eyes and cheeks, taking deep breaths as she did so.

At last, she looked at us. "Well? Will she hate me?"

Irritatingly enough, she looked even better for the flush in her white cheeks, and the dampness of her eyes made them glow in the moonlight. "She'll think you're lovely," I admitted.

At that, Madame Viart smiled. It was like the sun breaking through clouds. "Then let's meet the little hellion," she declared.

Jo exhaled audibly. I only shook my head and crawled back to the door, trying to ignore Madame Viart's bust brushing against my back. She had laced her stays very tight. *Stunning*, I had thought upon first seeing her in Medby, so long ago.

In Medby, with my father at my side.

Since we had first landed in Dormouth, there had been little opportunity to think on him. Now the grief came over me swiftly—and just as swiftly left. Would there come a day when his memory made me feel nothing? Would I thus lose him a second time?

"Are you unwell?" Madame Viart inquired. "It's perfectly understandable. I myself have been ill since I arrived in this wretched place."

"Nothing. Just a chill." I darted across the door to the far side, nodding at Jo. She reached over and rapped twice, her other hand going under her coat where the pistol rested. I made ready to draw my knife.

When the door opened, Jo ducked inside, then waved us in after her. Miss Morrow greeted us both warmly, but paused as Madame Viart appeared.

"Miss Morrow," Jo said, shutting the door, "this is our

French counterpart, Madame Viart. Madame Viart, this is Miss Morrow."

Miss Morrow, her mouth half-open, shut it again and instead looked thoughtfully at Madame Viart. "My brother has spoken of you," she said.

"And he has told me of you," Madame Viart replied, a tremor in her voice.

There was another pause, pregnant with meaning, and then Miss Morrow held out her hand. "I am pleased to make the acquaintance of someone Frannie thinks highly of."

I felt a knot in my stomach unwind. A glance at Jo showed she was equally relieved. It was no small pleasure to see the happy astonishment on Madame Viart's face, or that her hand trembled as she clasped Miss Morrow's.

"Now, to business," Miss Morrow continued. She gestured us to the two cots and we obediently sat down. "Whatever Missus Masterson is planning, it will begin before sunrise."

"So soon?" Jo exclaimed. "I thought we would at least have the morning."

"The festival will begin with a sunrise sermon that she will deliver personally from the beach where we came ashore. While she speaks, Penelope and I are to be rowed out into the bay, where we will place the circles on the surface of the water."

"And then?" I asked.

She shook her head. "When I asked, I was simply told to wait and see."

We all fell silent as the full import of her words became clear. So little time! I felt my fear rising again, a small, panicky voice telling me to take Jo and *run*.

"Is Miss Brocas coming back tonight?" Jo asked, bringing me back to the moment.

"I don't think so. She's dining at the castle, she said she had much to discuss with Missus Masterson and to not wait up for her. And I nearly forgot—! Forgive me." She lurched up again and opened a small cupboard, revealing bread, a platter with meat, cheeses, and salad, and a wine bottle. "As I didn't know how you were faring, I claimed to be ravenous."

Jo gave a cry of delight and took the platter from her.

"I only have two cups," she continued apologetically as she poured out wine. "Perhaps you two could share, and Madame could have the other?"

"What about you?" I asked, but she waved her hand.

"I already ate, and I have more work to do." She sat back down, flexing her long, fine fingers. "I still don't know what Missus Masterson intends, but two things have become clear: the symbols have to be precise, and the circles must be linked together." She strung an imaginary line in the air. "I tried making subtle alterations to the symbols but Penelope corrected me, and now the canvases are sealed with that—that slime. I don't think further amendments will affect them. However, I will next be attaching rawhide strips between the frames. I think I can make some of them loose, and then separate the circles once they're on the water, when it's too late to repair them."

"That's wonderful!" I exclaimed, while at the same time Madame Viart asked, "What's all this about circles? I thought we were leaving!"

Miss Morrow replied, "Leaving? Absolutely not. You might—"

"Enough," Jo cut in around a mouthful of salad. She swallowed and continued, "there is no time to explain to Madame about the paintings. As for leaving, the question is moot: the only bay calm enough to sail out of is the one below the village."

"But there must be a way!" Madame Viart cried, aghast. She rounded on me. "You must find a way to get me off this island. Myself and Mademoiselle Morrow."

"I am not leaving," Miss Morrow retorted. "I am seeing this through."

"But why in God's name do you want to stay?" Before Miss Morrow could reply, Madame Viart seized her hand. "You must understand: that woman is not right in her mind, and that monster is bigger than a ship! There is nothing we can do to stop it. We need a navy, we need warships, cannons—"

"Speaking of cannons," I interrupted gently, gratified when they both turned to me, each with their eyes flashing. Oh, together they would keep Mr. Morrow on his toes, if they survived to see him again.

They had to. We all had to.

"Madame Viart is right," I explained. "It will take a navy to defeat the monster. And the English navy, at least, is close by, but they cannot see our signal through the fog, nor what they are sailing into."

"Probably the reason for the fog in the first place," Jo put in. "Without our signal, they won't come until Monday. They wanted to give us time to assess the situation here."

"But we will be dead by Monday," Madame Viart said, enunciating each word.

"So, we will find a cannon, and more bluntly signal that

something is amiss," Miss Morrow said with a delighted expression.

"Exactly," Jo said, and I smiled to hear the note of pride in her voice. "I had thought to wait until the sun was up, in hopes they might glimpse our location. But we'll have to content ourselves with making an awfully loud bang."

"So why haven't you already done this?" Madame Viart demanded. "You have had all day!"

"Because the only cannons we have seen are in the castle," I said.

For a moment the two women pondered my words. "Few have been inside," Madame Viart said thoughtfully. "They say she's very private, they have the boy leave her deliveries at the gate."

"I can get in easily enough," Miss Morrow said.

"But do you know how to fire a cannon?" Jo asked, then looked at me, frowning. "For that matter, do you?"

I hesitated. "I … can load a pistol fairly well?"

When her gaze swung to Madame Viart, the latter shook her head. "Well then," Jo said. "It looks like it's me for the ramparts, while perhaps the rest of you create a diversion?"

"You cannot go up there alone," I said quickly—quickly, and a little loudly; I saw it in the others' faces. But it was suddenly there again, that looming fear: if we separated in that dread place and I lost her forever …

"Caroline," Jo said.

"I can help you," I rushed on. "You'll need help. Why, they have whole teams of men to operate cannons on ships."

"Let's you and I talk about that," Jo replied calmly. "Miss

Morrow, Madame Viart, can either of you think of some kind of distraction to cover my entrance?"

Miss Morrow tapped her chin. "Let me think on it."

"Also, has Miss Brocas said anything about a map, or about England and France being connected by land?" Jo asked. At Miss Morrow's astonished expression, she nodded at Madame Viart. "Missus Masterson had them hang a strange map in the tavern, showing England merged with the Continent."

"What an extraordinary idea," Miss Morrow exclaimed. "She has said nothing to me. I wonder what it means."

"It means that woman is ill in her mind," Madame Viart said firmly.

"It means something," Jo replied, her voice equally as firm. She rose, dusting off her breeches, and held her hand out to me.

I swallowed hard as I let her pull me up. This was what she had promised me: that we would decide together. But I kept remembering her words in Dormouth: *yes, this is the sensible plan; it may even be the only plan. But it's not right.*

She led me out into the pitch-dark larger room, closing the door behind us. "Caro, I'm as frightened as you are," she began. "If we can make it work that we both go up to the turret—"

"I made Madame Viart a promise," I burst out. I was suddenly on the verge of tears, everything rising up—Jo, my promise, my father. "In Medby. She wanted an open promise in exchange for getting me on the boat, she said she would think of something at a later date. Jo, I gave her my word. If she insists that I try to get her away—I should have told you, I'm so sorry—"

At once Jo was hugging me. "Bloody Viart," she breathed.

"It's all right, darling. Truly. And I don't think she's quite that foolish." She laughed softly into my hair. "If it helps any, I swore in my letter to Morrow that I would look after Helena personally, but that's not going to happen, is it?"

"I will look after her," I said thickly.

"You three will need to look after each other," she replied, her own voice shuddering. "Caro, if there was any other way … you know that, yes? If there was any other way."

"I know." I was weeping now. I felt sick inside, sick and lost. "You were right," I added through my tears. "We should have pushed her off the bloody boat and gone with her."

She laughed again and drew back a little to wipe at my face. "Is everything that dire, that it's driven my country girl to swear—"

But she broke off as we heard the sound of footsteps approaching the studio. Many footsteps. Quickly we returned to the smaller room, where Madame Viart had moved to one side of the window and positioned Miss Morrow opposite herself. Torchlight lit the glass as bright as sunrise and a voice called out, "Let us see, then, who conspires against me." My body shuddered violently, for I knew that voice all too well. I had last heard it shouting from a beach, in a painting. Mrs. Masterson had left her castle.

CHAPTER X

The Castle

We all went still at the sound of Mrs. Masterson's voice, as if her very inflections had the power to incapacitate us. Miss Morrow turned and peeked out the window, keeping herself hidden. "We must hide Miss Chase," she said. "There are too many of them to risk any other plan. This is our moment, we must not waste it."

I was trembling, trembling and icy cold, for the moment I had so dreaded was upon us, but I could not falter, for all our sakes. *Breathe, that's my girl.* "Where?" I asked, relieved when my voice sounded almost normal.

"In the studio. There's a covered hole in one corner. It looks like it was once used for storage. It smells decidedly unpleasant, but it could fit a person if they crouched down."

"Ladies," Stan shouted. "Would you come outside, please?"

"How do we know you won't shoot us on sight?" Madame Viart yelled back, waving her hand at us: *go on.*

"We'll play fair if you will."

I looked at Jo, trying to absorb every detail of her lovely face, to hold this moment. "Go," I said.

"Caro—"

"Go," I repeated, trying to somehow put into that one

word all my love. I held her eyes, willing her: *please don't make me say it a third time, I don't know if I can …*

She nodded. Her own lips were trembling, and she wiped roughly at her eyes. "Show me," she said to Miss Morrow.

They disappeared into the studio. I checked my knife; I rested my hand upon my chest and took slow, deep breaths. *In and out, in and out.* "We want safe passage off this island in the names of King Louis and King George," Madame Viart shouted.

At that, laughter rose up from outside, several voices all cackling merrily. "Unfortunately, those fellows hold little sway here," Stan called. "But we'll see about passage once we've had a chat."

"So, you want only to talk?" She looked at me. "I cannot do this for long," she whispered.

"Just until Miss Morrow returns," I whispered back. "We must try to stay together."

"Ladies, I think you need to come out, or we'll be forced to come in," Stan shouted.

"And then what?" Madame Viart demanded of me.

I shook my head. We had no arsenal, and even if we did, what would be the point? We were on an island, and who would the people believe: agents of the very lands they were fleeing, or their benefactor?

My body was still cold, my heart was racing beneath my hand so badly I felt lightheaded. I wanted nothing more than to run into the studio and seize Jo and never, ever, let her go.

Breathe, that's my girl. And I did.

Miss Morrow came back in, dusting her hands. "It's done," she said softly. "What do we do now?"

"Ladies, I am going to count—"

"We're coming!" Madame Viart yelled. Glaring at me, she added, "We surrender!" With a toss of her head, she went to the door and flung it open, revealing more torchlight, and many waiting figures.

Impulsively, I yanked the knife from my sleeve and tucked it into Miss Morrow's pocket. "If it gets found, say it was for cutting those strips," I whispered.

"They may even believe me," Miss Morrow replied drily, but I saw her hands were shaking as she followed Madame Viart.

With a last, longing look towards the studio—oh, my *darling*—I tore myself away and went outside to meet Mrs. Masterson.

A ring of more than a dozen people awaited us, some holding torches, the others with guns trained on us. In their center stood Stan and his two seconds, the former smirking as we emerged. Beside them was Mrs. Masterson, her head turned as she spoke to Miss Brocas. This was not the wild witch I had seen in the other Arcadia, however; this was an elegant, wealthy woman dressed as if for a ball. Her red damask dress glowed in the torchlight, her grey hair was elaborately curled, her face a mask of powder and rouge. On her breast was a large gold brooch of the familiar symbol of the Leviathan.

Miss Brocas ran forward and flung her arms around Miss Morrow. "Helena!" she cried. "Come away, quickly!"

Miss Morrow gave us an anxious look as she was led towards the ring of people. I nodded reassuringly and saw Madame Viart do the same. She faced far better odds with Miss Brocas protecting her.

"We're missing one," Stan said.

"Then you must find her," Mrs. Masterson replied. Her head swiveled to where Miss Brocas was leading Miss Morrow towards the castle. "Will you not present your pet to me, Penelope?"

At her words Miss Brocas froze, looking for all the world like a frightened deer. The people moved aside as Mrs. Masterson glided towards them; my own stomach knotted in sickening anticipation. She touched Miss Morrow under the chin, raising her face to the torchlight, revealing the naked revulsion on Miss Morrow's face. Her fingers felt Miss Morrow's jaw, then reached up to stroke her hair. I could feel a scream rising in my throat.

"Don't you touch her," Madame Viart barked. Such was the authority in her voice that Mrs. Masterson's hand stopped in mid-air, hovering beside Miss Morrow's head. "Or is it de rigueur to molest prisoners who have honorably surrendered?"

One of the men muttered to his fellow, who turned and whispered in Stan's ear, his expression disturbed. Mrs. Masterson hesitated a moment longer, her lip curling, but she took a step back; Miss Morrow visibly shuddered. "Such an asset should not be left unattended, Penelope," Mrs. Masterson said. "She stays with you until our work is complete."

And then she turned to us.

I heard Madame Viart hiss in surprise; for my part, it was all I could do to keep from screaming. Mrs. Masterson's eyes seemed entirely black, with only the thinnest line of white on either side of her irises. She took a long look at each of us in turn, and when her gaze settled on me my gorge rose, so foul was the impression she made.

"Take off your hat," she purred.

Slowly I removed my hat and her lips curled into an awful smile. "I knew you would return," she continued in the same purring voice. "And you have brought me my son's whore. We are blessed in our purpose."

A murmur went up among the people ranged around her, and a few crossed themselves.

"What are you going to do with us?" Madame Viart demanded.

"Come and find out," Mrs. Masterson said. Her followers closed in around us, making it clear that we had no choice. Behind us, men slipped into the studio. I could only hope that they would not find Jo.

We were marched through a copse of trees to the castle wall. Here we came to a narrow moat, long since drained and grassed over, then across a new wooden drawbridge into the bailey. The dim space kept shifting in the flickering torch-light, now showing the windows of the keep, now smothering all details into hulking shadow. In the middle of the bailey was a rectangular pool that ran to the seaward wall, where it ended in an arched gate with a lowered portcullis. Opaque water lapped within the pool, echoing off the walls, mimicking the sea that fed into it.

Mrs. Masterson strode to the pool and sat beside it, trailing her arm in the water, singing under her breath. A gun at my back nudged Madame Viart and I close to her.

As we watched, a tentacle as thick as an oar slithered up Mrs. Masterson's arm and twined around it, followed by a second and a third. Somewhere behind us Miss Morrow cried out in fright, but I could only watch, my nauseating fear giving way to a blessed numbness.

"See how they love me as a mother," she said, looking at us with those bottomless eyes. "See how they know me for their god."

"Where is their true mother?" I blurted out, ignoring Madame Viart's hiss. I could not say what made me so bold. Weariness, that this absurd nightmare would not end? Or perhaps my growing conviction that none of us would get out of this alive?

At my words Mrs. Masterson flinched, then her lip curled again. "What would a tribade and a whore know of motherhood?" she asked. "I have buried two sons because of your pathetic meddling. But this time you are too late. The die is cast, and I will do what no man in history has dared."

Before I could respond, Madame Viart yawned dramatically. "Always talking," she said with a sneer. "Thomas talked too. All day long he would talk about his power, his glory. His, his, his. He put me to sleep, and you are putting me to sleep."

Mrs. Masterson's lip curled. "Stanley," she said.

I saw Stan look at his fellows, then step forward. "Yes, ma'am."

"Yes, Stan, obey her," Madame Viart continued in the same sneering tone. A nervous, yet furious energy radiated from her. "Obey her while you can, for soon it will be your turn." She pointed at the pond. "How long before you become their supper? How long before all of you are fed to the big one? Or hasn't she told you about the big one, the grown-up one? How it's larger than a frigate, how it wrecked both the French and English navies, how it eats men like a child eating sweets?"

Alarmed whispers filled the air as she spoke, and at last I understood Madame Viart's motives: these people had no idea where these creatures came from, or what they would soon become. Mrs. Masterson got to her feet, shaking off the tentacles. Squealing sounds filled the bailey at her absence. "Stanley," she said calmly, "shoot her."

"No!" Miss Morrow cried out, only to be hushed by Miss Brocas.

Stan's expression was unreadable. "Begging your pardon, Missus Masterson," he said, "but you're not thinking right. If we're attacked—"

"I gave you an order," she snapped.

"If we're attacked by either side we'll need them," he pressed. The others murmured in uneasy assent. "Two spies, two *women*, are damn useful hostages. I've seen some pretty high up officers come to the table just to get a spy back. That, plus the stir women prisoners would cause back home? We'll have real bargaining power."

"What do I care about officers?" Mrs. Masterson demanded, visibly astonished. "What do I care about petty kings and their petty demands? I told you to shoot her!"

Stan grimaced. I watched him take a breath, then begin again, "Ma'am, they surrendered and came as we asked. It's not right to shoot a prisoner in cold—"

As he was speaking, Mrs. Masterson crossed the distance between them in a few short strides, seized a pistol from another man, and shot Stan in the head.

Everyone screamed then. I screamed, Madame Viart screamed, Miss Morrow screamed, many of our captors screamed; the creatures in the pond screeched and wailed and I fell to my knees and covered my ears with my hands. *Jo*, I thought wildly, *Jo, Jo!* I wanted her there so I could throw myself in her arms and I wanted her to live, to run as far as she could from this terrible place.

Mrs. Masterson walked up to the body and nudged it with her foot. "Well?" she said, looking around the bailey, her voice ringing out over the cacophony. "Can any of you follow orders, or must I shoot her myself?"

The cries and weeping swiftly tapered off into silence. No one moved. From among the others, I heard a muffled sob, followed by hushing.

With a sigh, Mrs. Masterson bent over, her panniers swaying around her hips, and seized Stan's rifle. Bracing a foot on his stomach, she wrenched it from his dead body and pointed it at Madame Viart.

"No!" Madame Viart cried. I lurched upright and ran to her. I could not even think, I only knew I had to somehow stop this.

A white, wailing blur threw itself at Mrs. Masterson's feet. Her sobs were taken up by the creatures in the pool again, a shrieking chorus that set my ears ringing once more.

"Don't shoot!" Penelope Brocas screamed, flinging her arms around Mrs. Masterson's skirts. "I cannot bear it!"

"Get out of my way," Mrs. Masterson snarled, trying to shove her aside and steady the rifle at the same time.

"You mustn't, you mustn't!" The young woman's face was wild with a terrible grief I could barely look at. I seized Madame Viart's hand and her icy fingers gripped mine painfully. "I cannot bear it, I'll go mad! Oh God I want to die, shoot me instead, let me die, I want to die …"

With a cry of frustration Mrs. Masterson swung the rifle butt into Miss Brocas's face. The shrieking litany became a moan as the young woman tumbled backwards, clutching at her head. She curled into a ball as Mrs. Masterson began kicking her, kicking and kicking her thin little body until Miss Brocas was nothing more than a heap of fabric and twisted limbs.

"For God's sake, stop!" Miss Morrow cried out, openly weeping. "She's just a girl!"

Abruptly Mrs. Masterson stopped. She stared down at the limp body, then held out the rifle. One of Stan's seconds rushed forward and took it. "Take Penelope to her room," she said. "Make sure she is able to fulfill her duty tomorrow." She looked around at the little crowd, as if seeing us all for the first time. "Put the pet in with her," she added.

I exhaled and felt Madame Viart do the same. Miss Morrow looked at us as she was hurried past, her gaze hollow, then bent over the Miss Brocas as they disappeared into the keep. She would be safe until tomorrow, and tomorrow might just be enough.

If Jo was caught—if Jo was already dead—

"As for you two." We both straightened as Mrs. Masterson

approached. Violence had caused her white face to blotch lividly beneath the powder, distorting her features in the torch-light. Her hand flashed out to strike Madame Viart. I barely registered the gleam of metal in her palm before Madame Viart fell to her knees howling, her hands pressed over her face. As I bent over her I saw blood running between her fingers. I tried to prise her hands free but she twisted away from me, wailing and howling into her palms.

"What did you do?" I cried.

"Thomas wrote to me all about his little French bird." Mrs. Masterson's voice was toneless. "What a rare beauty she was, how much she pleased him. Better that she meets her maker with a face that matches her soul." She wiped a piece of curved metal on her skirts, the blood indistinguishable from the red damask. "You, Philip. Take these two to the cells. I want them on the beach before dawn. The rest of you come with me."

Men came and seized us. I cried out again as they roughly yanked Madame Viart to her feet. She seemed almost insensible to what was happening, only moaning into her hands as they dragged her towards the far side of the bailey. "Please," I said, twisting to look at my captors. "Please let me stay with her. We have but a few hours to live, please let me comfort her."

One of the men hushed me, and I realized he had been one of Stan's seconds. His face was ashen and damp with sweat, though the night air was cool. If I had said something to Jo back in Dormouth about Stan, if I had been more attuned to what was around me rather than wallowing in my fears?

"I'm sorry, miss," he said, then mouthed, *not here.*

I felt a twinge of hope as I was marched after Madame Viart, their hands like iron on my arms. Halfway across the bailey, we heard voices behind us, and the terrible squealing cries rose up again. We stopped as one and looked back at the pool. Two men were stripping Stan's clothes off him with practiced swiftness as tentacles slithered over the edge and waved in the air in perverse supplication. When Stan's poor moonlit body was naked, they seized him by his arms and legs and swung him into the water. The bailey filled with the sounds of wet flesh slapping and twining. Sprays of water shot up into the night sky, catching the moonlight like jewels.

"Stan, you poor bastard," the man said aloud, and I was dragged into the depths of the castle.

CHAPTER XI

The Final Night

We were taken into one of the corner turrets and up a floor. Here were several barred cells, following the curve of the thick stone walls, the whole gloomy and damp. Only a single torch illuminated our surroundings. Ahead of me, Madame Viart was dragged into a cell, and when I tried to follow her, I was instead shoved into the next one.

"Please," I begged. "You are Philip, aren't you?" At his uneasy nod I pressed, "Philip, please let me stay with her. She shouldn't be alone now."

Philip shut the barred door and locked it, then he leaned in close. "Miss, I have my orders," he said in a low voice. "I've got a wife and babe here. I cannot risk their lives. I'm sorry."

"None of us will be safe come dawn!" I cried as he turned away. "At least see to her wound. Ease her suffering in these last hours, I beg of you."

He shook his head. "You ought to be careful how you plead, miss. Some fellows might want to see just how far you're willing to go for your friend."

"Robbie's a neat hand for stitches," another of the men said. I could not see him or the others, but I felt a rush of goodwill towards him as he spoke. "I'd trust my own woman's face to him, not that I'd let some harpy cut her."

"Be quiet," Philip said sharply. He glanced at me again with an unreadable expression. "Fetch Robbie, then. And some hot water," he added.

"Thank you," I called after him as he strode back to the stairs. "Thank you."

When they had left, I pressed against the bars, trying to see into Madame Viart's cell. "Madame," I whispered loudly. "Madame, they are bringing someone to help you."

My words were met with silence save for her shuddering breaths.

"We may yet survive this," I continued. "Please let them help you. We will need all our wits when dawn comes. Please, Madame. Think of Miss Morrow, think of her brother."

At the latter there came a mournful wail, so riddled with pain that tears of sympathy sprang to my eyes. I reached through the bars, hoping I might touch her, let her know she wasn't alone.

But then footsteps hurried up the stairs and three men came in, making straight for Madame Viart. One of them, I hoped, was the neat-handed Robbie. Between the three of them they were carrying towels, a bowl of steaming water, and a leather case.

They went into her cell, speaking to her in soft voices. I couldn't make out what they were saying, or if Madame Viart responded. I only knew they had begun when she started screaming.

My own tears began to fall, and then came the unholy shrieking from the pool, as if the creatures too were somehow sympathetic to Madame Viart's plight. I went to the tiny window of my cell, a mere slit in the wall, and peered down into the bailey. The surface of the water was heaving and swirling; tentacles felt along the top of the portcullis like so many grasping fingers. Blood still stained the stone paving. Madame Viart cried out again, a scream that trailed off into a sob, and as if summoned, one of the creatures broke the surface and screamed in turn. As repulsive, as harrowing as its cry was, I could not help but liken it to a child crying for its mother.

I lost track of time, then. The men left; small, animal noises came from Madame Viart's cell, but she would not respond to my concern and soon fell silent. I hoped she was resting; I hoped the stitches would ultimately ease her suffering. The towels they carried out had been deeply stained with blood. I had not realized cuts could bleed so much, but what did I know of such things?

Then I remembered my poor mother, and all the blood of that final morning; I remembered the man I had killed; and I realized I knew a little after all.

Breathe, my girl. In and out, in and out.

Not that it mattered any longer. If Jo had succeeded, we should have heard the cannon by now. There had been nothing save the lapping of the water, the pacing of a guard across the bailey. Nothing save our impending doom.

A great rush of grief and fear filled me. This was the one

thing I had feared above all else. I shoved my fist in my mouth, that Madame Viart might not hear my wracking sobs. All I had asked was to have Jo by my side—oh, selfish, selfish! Perhaps she had escaped, perhaps she had been dispatched cleanly, without even time to note the deed. Yet I *wanted* her, I wanted her. The pain of her absence made me insensible to all else, there was only a torrent of agonizing sorrow—

And then it ebbed, just a little, and I was still there.

Breathe, that's my girl.

I took a breath, and another, pressing my hand to my chest, imagining it was not my own but my father's. That comforting weight. Tears were streaming down my face, my breath was coming in choking gulps—but I felt my tears, I heard my breath again.

Well. If I could not have the mercy of Jo beside me, I could at least have some say in my death. I could perhaps wield my life as a weapon, should it come to such.

The thought calmed me further. I wiped at my face, then placed a hand on my chest once more, letting the pressure slow my shuddering breaths. *In and out, in and out.* Oh, I had hoped Jo and I would face this time together—but I had also believed I would be by my father's side when he passed. All my efforts to sway events, all my hopes and wishes and pleas, had come to naught. So be it. Stan was dead and Madame Viart was maimed and in all likelihood, the violence had just begun.

The wracking grief came over me once more, but this time I did not lose my senses to it. This time I managed to breathe through the contortions.

When I quieted this time, I heard a different sound—no, a series of sounds, like a murmuring voice. "Madame?" I said, hurrying back to the barred door.

"Are you there? Are you hurt?" Her voice was a croak, barely comprehensible. Fresh tears welled in my eyes.

"I'm here," I said, then, flushing with shame, "I am unhurt." I worked my hand through the bars and pushed my arm as far as it would go, and was rewarded with her plump, bloodstained hand reaching out in turn. We were just able to hook our fingers around each other's. The simple contact, the feel of her sandpapery skin: in that moment it seemed nothing short of miraculous.

"There has been no cannon," she said then, her voice a little stronger.

"No," I managed to reply.

"And your lover isn't here."

"No," I said again, only it came out close to a sob, and I clapped my free hand over my mouth while I forced the tears back.

A deep sigh came from the other cell and her fingers squeezed mine. "I am sorry, Caroline."

How did she know my name? But that, too, did not matter anymore. "If you are to call me Caroline, I should return the favor," I said with a shuddering laugh.

"You English spies are such amateurs," she said, but there was no malice in it, only a kind of wistfulness. "I am Elinor. But only for a few. For everyone else I remain Madame Viart." Before I could reply, she continued, "I want to warn you now. Whatever they do to us, wherever they take us, I am going to kill that woman, and with luck I shall die myself. Don't try to stop me. I am telling you this so I do not have to kill you too."

I waited a beat, trying to think on how to respond; and then I began carefully, "What of Miss Morrow—"

"Oh, she is like Francis, that one," Madame Viart said with a little laugh. "She will survive, no matter the odds." Then, more coldly, "That woman cut my *face*. I survived my monstrous Papa, I survived marriage to that brute Viart, I survived the gutter and the brothel and I became a mistress and a spy and men came to *me* then, they *crawled* to me if I wished it. All from this face. And she, she *took* that from me …" The rest of her words were lost in a violent sob.

My heart broke anew at her outburst. How had I thought so little of her, how had I cringed at the thought of being beholden to her? I squeezed her fingers as best I could, trying to put all my sympathy, all my comfort, into that one gesture. "Madame—Elinor—your injury is not the sum of you. I know you're in terrible pain, but it has not changed who you are, or what you have accomplished."

"You would not understand," she replied in a sodden voice. "I don't expect you to understand. Only do not get in my way."

But that was not true. I did understand, or at least I thought I did. For just a moment I let myself think of Jo again, of her and my father when we were together, together and *happy*—

"If Jo has truly failed," I said, "then I will help you to kill her."

And tensed, waiting for the sharp retort, the sneering dismissal, but there was only a shaky inhale that told me she was weeping again. "Very well," she whispered at last. "We will end her. Only I am not to be saved, do you understand? I cannot bear to go on like this, I cannot bear anyone to *see*—"

Madame Viart broke off in a fit of coughing, as did I. Air had gusted through our little windows, a different kind of air.

"Fire," I cried. "But where?"

An explosion made us both jump. The sound echoed in our cells, making my ears ring painfully. There was a second, smaller boom, and then a series of little pops, like gunfire. Shouts went up outside. I ran to my window, hope blossoming in my chest, watching people dart to and fro in the bailey. There were cries for water, for guns; voices demanded if we were under attack. At last, a man shouted for quiet.

"That was the gunpowder store," he bellowed. "We have a traitor in our midst. I want everyone to separate into parties and search the island. And be ready for anything—there could be more than one."

The people quickly grouped themselves and ran out the gate. For a moment I hoped—but no, two men were directed towards our tower, rifles at the ready. Across, in the keep, candles were being lit.

"Do you think it was her?" Madame Viart called. I guessed she was standing at her own window.

"I hope so," I replied, trying to keep the frantic hope from my voice. *Oh, let it be Jo. Oh, let her be all right …*

"She's cleverer than I thought. Maybe she will burn the whole island down."

"Or just create enough disturbance to reach our navy."

"How long before they might come?"

I hesitated, trying to think. It was still dark outside. Would the sound have carried far enough? Could they glimpse the glow of a fire through the fog? "I don't know," I began, "but we should be ready—"

I fell silent as footsteps echoed on the stairs once more. Philip appeared, flanked by three other brawny fellows. This time, he was also accompanied by two women. They held piles of white cloth in their arms.

"You are both to change and come with me," he said. "It's time."

CHAPTER XII

The Final Dawn

I changed clothes under the watchful eye of a grim-faced woman, the men standing armed just outside my cell. The dress was of roughly woven white cloth and hung as shapeless as a nightshirt. Without the layers of my suit I was suddenly chilled, or was it fear? I was allowed to keep my stockings and shoes, and my wrists were encased in thin, discreet manacles. The woman pinned a rosebud to my breast, red as blood against the white.

"Do you really think it will stop at just us?" I asked the woman as she worked the pins through the stem. "It will kill everyone and take half the island with it."

"I don't know what you mean," the woman muttered.

"The Leviathan. The parent of those creatures in the water below. The monster that I watched break a frigate in two."

"You're mad," the woman snapped, but her expression was uneasy.

"Then why these clothes?" I pressed. Madame Viart had already planted the seeds. If I could provoke enough doubt, alert enough of them to what was coming … "We are to be *sacrificed*. Her sons did the same, they fed it dozens of women and enslaved people—"

The woman slapped me, so hard that lights burst in my eye. I could not help my whimper of pain. "That's enough," she said sharply. "You ought to be ashamed, spouting such nonsense. You're lucky she hasn't had you shot for spying. That's what they do to spies, did you know that? My brother was shot for it, and we got nothing from His Majesty for our loss, nothing. All you have to do is look nice on the beach, so the others aren't alarmed. Afterwards she'll give you back to your people."

At the absurdity of this proposition I could only laugh, which earned me another slap. I came out in the hall with my eyes tearing from the blows.

And then I saw the long, ugly caterpillar of stitching that marred Madame Viart's pristine cheek, and I wept again. "Oh, Madame," I gasped. "I'm so, so sorry."

Though her own eyes were full, she raised her chin and her lip curled into that familiar sneer. "Save your sympathy for *her*. She'll need it far more than I."

"None of that," Philip ordered, and I saw that he was once more in charge of us. At least we might have one captor willing to listen, when matters came to a crisis.

We were led out into the bailey. It was that darkest hour before dawn, and a chill wind stirred the lingering wisps of smoke. I could hear the surf beyond the castle walls. We were immediately hemmed in by a dozen armed men, none of whom would meet our eyes—or look at all at Madame Viart's face. Her grim expression deepened with every avoidance.

The door to the keep opened, and three more women in white emerged: Miss Brocas, her face visibly battered, her skin beneath the bruises so pale it matched her dress; Miss Morrow, seemingly unharmed; and behind them both, Mrs. Masterson. Though she also wore white, her dress was oddly fashioned, little more than a sleeveless tunic. Her wiry arms were bared to the night, as were her feet beneath the folds of the skirt. To complete her costume, she wore a belt around her waist from which hung a large sword.

Miss Morrow's eyes found mine and I saw her visibly sag in relief—and then her expression became sorrowful when she saw Madame Viart. She touched her cheek, then laid her hand over her heart; Madame Viart made a small noise and turned away, dabbing at her eyes with one manacled hand.

Again, Miss Morrow looked at me, raising her arms to show her wrists. I mimicked the gesture, showing my manacles. In response she tapped her hip; it took me a moment to remember the knife I had put it in her pocket. Had she somehow managed to bring it despite the thin gown? I nodded, hoping I understood her gesture, then mouthed *are you hurt* and felt my own rush of relief when she shook her head—cut short when Miss Brocas said something to her and Miss Morrow looked away.

At a signal from Mrs. Masterson, we processed out of the castle and up the path we had come only the day before. Inland, I could see a gleam among the trees, as if a large fire was still smoldering. Smoke trailed up into the night sky. Could Mr. Smith and his men have seen it? Surely they must have heard it? Unless they were too far away, unless …

A shout came from the path ahead, and a man jogged down to meet us. He conferred with Mrs. Masterson, who signaled one of the women to come to her. There was another exchange and the woman hurried back towards the castle.

Before we reached the village we turned left and found ourselves descending a series of steep switchbacks to the beach. Of necessity we slowed, some linking arms as they navigated the narrow path. Below us, waves lapped relentlessly against the shore. The western horizon was still purple-black, too dark to distinguish sky from sea from fog. Ahead, a fellow twisted his ankle and cursed loudly, yet Mrs. Masterson did not break her stride, moving surefooted down to the rocky sand.

On the beach, a platform had been built, with a little railing all around dripping with roses. I wondered where they had come from, for we had not seen a single bush, then shook my head wryly: the monster would soon be upon us, yet here I was musing on the whereabouts of a rose bush. Should I not be praying, consigning my soul to God? But I was still my father's daughter, and he had never placed great store in rituals of faith. *A good father*, he would say, *can hear his children however they choose to speak.* The only thing I would pray for would be to see Jo one last time.

Near the platform, two dinghies had been drawn up. The canvas circles were stacked and tied to one of them, and now three men began working the boat into the surf. With a last look at me, Miss Morrow climbed into the other, followed by Miss Brocas. As they were pushed out to sea by more men, Miss Morrow tapped her hip again.

"I think the hellion has a plan," I whispered to Madame Viart.

"Unless it's a plan to kill that woman, I do not care,"

Madame Viart whispered back. "Will you help me or not?"

"Only if you wait." I met her glare with one of my own. "If Miss Morrow can disrupt matters it increases our odds."

"Hmph." But she said no more.

I watched as the boats were rowed out into the placid bay. The men began pushing the circles onto the water, unfolding them like an accordion as they did. From the other boat, the white-clad women steered them into place while their oarsmen steadied the vessel. Silently, I willed Miss Morrow to be careful. The first cry from Miss Brocas could be her undoing.

Mrs. Masterson stepped into place before the platform, facing the sheer hillside behind us. I followed her gaze up and saw the Arcadians gathering at the top of the steps, many of them holding roses. Did they not think to question any of it? Or was it as Madame Viart had described, were they merely humoring the whim of their aged benefactor?

A woman placed a book in Mrs. Masterson's hand with a curtsey. A Bible, I guessed by the dense text. Opening it to a well-worn place, she seemed about to speak when a voice cried:

"Caro!"

I whirled about to see two men dragging yet another white-clad figure to the beach, a third pacing beside them with a gun drawn. Tears sprang to my eyes. Could it be that we would be together after all? Oh, I could face anything with Jo at my side.

"Caro," Jo called. "Together!"

The men tried to push her onto her knees in the sand, but she lunged towards me, her eyes wide in her soot-spattered face. She had taken two good steps when the third man swung his arm wide and struck her in the head with his gun.

Jo dropped like a stone.

I screamed then. I knew it was no killing blow, but she was at their mercy and I could do nothing.

"You scream at kindness?" Mrs. Masterson pointed at the still heap of Jo's body. "I could have had her shot in the woods and you would have never known her fate. Now you will witness the miracle together. I had no such moment with my sons."

"Because they were murderers," I gasped. "Because they were bent on their own power, because they thought only of conquering England." I smiled then despite my tears. "They never so much as mentioned you existed."

At that her face lit up, as if pleasantly surprised by a child. "That is true: they were limited in their ambitions. All their father's doing, of course. Instilling these strange notions of king and country, when there was a greater prize in reach." Suddenly she craned her head up, surveying the sky, then nodded to herself. "It is time," she said.

"You cannot control it," I cried as she turned away. "No one can. It will destroy the island. It will kill us all."

"Little fool," she said with a glance over her shoulder, "who ever said anything about controlling it?"

I stared at her, aghast, and then I was lunging for her before I could think, my manacled hands outstretched—

Only to find myself yanked back by Philip onto the wooden platform, skidding painfully to my knees. He struck me, but the blow was glancing. I feigned agony and doubled over. Madame Viart touched my shoulder in sympathy, but I knew she would not risk more until her opening came. She was biding her time for her revenge, and both Jo and Miss Morrow were vulnerable. I glanced through my sheltering arms at Philip, but his face was impassive. If we had any hope of surviving this I had to think of *something*.

But there was no more time to think. Mrs. Masterson bade a man bearing a torch to stand beside her, raised up her Bible, and began to read.

How can I describe the awfulness of that reciting voice, the sense of dread anticipation that seemed to crush the very breath of my body? The night sky was reddening, that first herald of the dawn, revealing the perpetual scrim of fog. Above us on the headland, the crowd of Arcadians was growing, some of the women holding sleeping babes. All bowed their heads as Mrs. Masterson read in a booming voice:

> *Then answered the Lord unto Job out of the whirlwind, and said,*
>
> *Gird up thy loins now like a man: I will demand of thee, and declare thou unto me.*
>
> *Wilt thou also disannul my judgment? wilt thou condemn me, that thou mayest be righteous?*
>
> *Hast thou an arm like God? or canst thou thunder with a voice like him?*
>
> *Deck thyself now with majesty and excellency; and array thyself with glory and beauty.*

Cast abroad the rage of thy wrath: and behold every one that is proud, and abase him.

Look on every one that is proud, and bring him low; and tread down the wicked in their place.

Hide them in the dust together; and bind their faces in secret.

Then will I also confess unto thee that thine own right hand can save thee.

Past her erect form I saw the two dinghies being steered around the circles of canvas. All were floating now. Miss Brocas nearly fell into the sea as she nudged them further and further apart, working them into the larger pattern I remembered from the diagram, like a vast necklace floating on the sea. Miss Morrow was bent over the far end of the dinghy, her back to the oarsman in the middle. I saw the flash of metal in her hand—

But then the men dragged Jo onto the platform. Her hair was matted with blood around a terrible bruising weal on her forehead, yet her eyes fluttered open and focused on me.

"Together," she whispered.

"Together," I agreed, smiling through my tears.

The sky lightened further, blotting out all but the last few stars. Above us, the Arcadians burst into song:

Soldiers of Christ, Arise, and put your armour on,
Strong in the strength which God supplies through His eternal Son.

Beneath their singing I heard something else, something I did not understand but recognized all the same. Mrs. Masterson had tossed the Bible aside as if it were nothing more than a cheap novel. Now she spread her bare arms, her lips spitting out those familiar, terrible sounds.

Behind her the surf grew choppy. The dinghies rocked wildly, and what had been gently lapping waves became a crashing surf that rolled thunderously onto the beach, leaving ribbons of foam in its wake.

"We need these manacles off," Jo hissed.

"Not likely," Madame Viart said from above us. "They still think her merely eccentric."

"You must be joking." Jo looked up, wincing as her forehead creased—or perhaps it was the sight of Madame Viart's stitches, now livid in the sunlight. "Bloody hell, Viart. I am sorry."

"Not as sorry as she will be."

From the castle, the Leviathan's offspring began to screech and wail. The hymn faltered, but a few strong voices carried them through the disruption:

Stand then against your foes, in close and firm array;
Legions of wily fiends oppose throughout the evil day.
But meet the sons of night, and mock their vain design,
Armed in the arms of heavenly light, of righteousness divine.

The bay exploded upwards through the ring of circles, sending a great plume of water into the air; across the whole of the visible sea the water was churning and swirling. I saw Miss Morrow and Miss Brocas cling to their dinghy, their faces upturned in astonishment, and then with a cry, Miss Morrow flung herself forward and began hacking at the nearest circle. The oarsman seized her arm and wrenched her backwards and Miss Brocas tried to separate them, all three struggling.

Still Mrs. Masterson kept up the awful chanting. The rising surf crashed against the beach, dousing us all in spray. Another plume rose up, up, higher than the headland, and rained down upon us and the Arcadians alike, causing them to exclaim in surprise and fear.

I helped Jo stagger to her feet, then rounded on Philip. "For God's sake," I said. "There's no more time. We have to stop her before it comes!"

He was shaking his head, his wide eyes fixed upon the water. "I cannot, I cannot," he whispered. "Oh, dear God, she owns this island ..."

"On three," Jo said in my ear. "You go after her. Madame and I will hold him off." She looked at Madame Viart and held up three fingers. Madame Viart nodded.

Two fingers. One. Then, in my ear, "Go!"

I ran towards Mrs. Masterson, drenched in sea water yet still reciting, her eyes raised to the sky and her arms outstretched. I dropped my shoulder, as Mr. Windham had shown me all those months ago, and slammed it into her chest.

She flew backwards into the surf. Out in the bay, Miss Brocas screamed. I was about to throw myself on Mrs. Masterson again when an arm wrapped around my neck and wrenched me away. I elbowed and kicked at Philip behind me. With a cry, Jo threw herself atop him, looping her manacled wrists around his neck. We all three tumbled painfully onto the rocky sand.

I looked up, gasping for air, and found myself staring at the shadowed form of Madame Viart. She plunged her arm into our tangled bodies and when she raised her hand again it was clutching a pistol. Philip cried out, "No!" as she calmly took aim at Mrs. Masterson and fired.

A massive tentacle erupted from the surf and slapped Madame Viart, sending her flying across the beach as if she were little more than a doll.

In silent accord we three stopped fighting, our gazes fixed upon the bay. Cold seawater sluiced over us, momentarily blinding us, and when the surf drew back again it kept drawing back, back, revealing more tentacles, each as thick as a man was tall. Back and up now, like a body rising beneath a sheet, the shadow of the swell falling over us. From above people were screaming, the young were screaming in the castle, we three were screaming.

The water broke in a great thunderous cascade, sending up clouds of mist and smashing the two dinghies to pieces. Jo cried out again, a pained, "No!" as we watched Miss Morrow and Miss Brocas tumble beneath the waves.

"My God," Philip chanted breathlessly beside me. "My God, my God."

I just stared, my throat raw and my body numb, as before us rose the Leviathan, blotting out the sky, the canvas circles still clinging to its head like a child's flower crown.

CHAPTER XIII

Leviathan

*G*reen-black tentacles slapped down on either side of us, spraying us with sand and pebbles, crushing screaming men beneath their terrible weight. The Leviathan heaved itself forward, its massive bulk sending up violent waves. Here was the gaping mouth ringed with sharp teeth that I had hoped to never see again; here were the staring yellow eyes that had haunted my dreams since that first dinner party with Edward Masterson, long ago. From the headland came the crackling of rifle shot but the volleys did not so much as make it twitch.

Mrs. Masterson bellowed a command at the monster. As it slid a tentacle towards her, she drew her sword free and held it aloft. The tentacle coiled around her legs and lifted her into the air. With her white gown plastered to her body, the sword catching the rising sun, and her grey hair streaming loose, she looked for all the world like a goddess of death. A small part of my mind thought, here was the true horror of the world: not the shadowy fears of children's tales, but human monsters standing in daylight, hiding nothing, fearing nothing.

Again, the rifles fired. In response, a tentacle punched the hillside, its tip coiled like a fist, raining people and debris

onto the beach below. Almost as an afterthought, the creature snatched up a screaming man and slung him into its
half-submerged maw. The snapping of its jaws was louder
than any shot. Out of the corner of my eye I saw two more
men fall to their knees and cross themselves.

A hand seized my forearm and I looked up to see Philip
unlocking my manacles. Jo was already on her feet, rubbing
her chafed wrists, her head swiveling as she tried to assess our
circumstances. It was almost too much to take in: the Leviathan
delicately placing Mrs. Masterson atop its head, the people being
hauled up from where they clung to the sheered hillside while a
panicked clamor echoed above, Madame Viart staggering to her
feet far down the beach, and in the churning sea—

"Look," I cried, leaping to my feet. "It's Miss Morrow!"

Her head went back under for a moment; and then she
broke the surface again, shaking spray from her face. She
seized a piece of the broken dinghy, then pulled a pale, limp
form against herself. Miss Brocas.

"We have to get them ashore," Jo said, turning to Philip.
"You must get everyone to move inland. Rifles are useless,
and one swipe of that beast will cause another landslide."

Keening cries rose up again from the castle, and then I
saw it: the Leviathan jerked as if bodily struck, its vast yellow
eyes swiveling towards the noise. Only when Mrs. Masterson
yelled at it did it turn its gaze back to the beach.

"Its young," I whispered. Could they challenge Mrs. Masterson's sway over the monster? I seized Philip's arm to get his
attention. "The ones in the castle. Can you raise the portcullis and release them?"

He just stared at me, his lips working soundlessly. I realized he might be in shock. "The young ones in the pool," I repeated more slowly. "Is there a way to release them?"

"Wait, you saw its young?" Jo whirled me about. "How many hatched?"

"Three, perhaps?" I tried to think, but all I could think on was Stan's body, and the blood running through Madame Viart's fingers.

"Release them and in a short time we'll have three more to deal with. We have to kill them."

I shook my head. Though her words made perfect sense, it *felt* wrong, only I couldn't think of how to explain.

Nor would I get a chance to, for just then came a whistling sound, followed by a meaty thud. The Leviathan roared, its damp, fetid breath blowing over us, and spun about in the water, sending up another wave that knocked us to our knees. When again I could see, there was a second whistling, and a third. The remaining Arcadians were shouting and pointing at the fog line—

—where a ship was breaking through flying the pennant of England, with another ship's prow emerging behind it.

"About bloody time!" Jo cried.

"Arcadians!" Mrs. Masterson held her sword aloft. "Arcadians, the time has come! Remember your vows! Defend this land with your lives!"

She swung the sword in a wide arc to point before herself. In an uncanny mirror of her gesture, the Leviathan swung a tentacle in a low, wide slap, sending up a massive spray of water that crashed over the ship. Before the ship was righted it slapped an opposite tentacle onto the water, rocking the ship violently the other way. And again, and again, while a third and fourth tentacle snatched sailors from the deck and tossed them into its mouth like a dog catching scraps.

Miss Morrow, gamely kicking both herself and Miss Brocas towards the beach, disappeared beneath the waves but just as quickly reappeared, Miss Brocas's yellow head limp against hers.

Jo was pulling off her boots. "We've got to help Miss Morrow before it returns," she said, then nodded at Philip. "You *must* move everyone back. It could collapse the entire headland."

He nodded, but his face was grey with fear and his eyes kept drifting to the back of the beast, where Mrs. Masterson stood aloft like some perverse charioteer, still waving her sword.

"Philip! Are you listening?"

He swallowed visibly, but his gaze focused on Jo once more.

"Good. Once you've got the others to a safe distance, see if you can signal any other ships from the northern end of the island. Start a fire, or try to row out past the fog line." She looked grimly at the bay, where the Leviathan had set the second ship spinning like a top. "It's like lambs to the slaughter. They can only hear the fight, they cannot see what they're sailing into."

With a last nod Philip took off running. I yanked off my own shoes. "Where is Madame Viart?" I gasped.

We looked around, then Jo angled her head at the steps. "There. What is she doing?"

Her little white form was gesturing at the top of the steps, her manacled hands upraised and waving towards herself: *to me, to me.* After a moment a man leaned over and dropped a rifle down into her waiting hands.

"You know, I like her better and better," Jo remarked, pushing her wet hair out of her face. "Quickly, now."

I pulled off my own shoes and waded out into the icy surf after her. Miss Morrow caught sight of us and adjusted her direction accordingly, but even from a distance I could tell she was exhausted. Beneath my stockinged feet the sand dipped quickly, and ahead of me, Jo was a mere head and shoulders above the churning water. This was not the sea as I knew it in the north: this was bluer water, made opaque by bubbles and clouds of silt. I could not see my feet, could only hope that we could get the women onto dry land quickly, before the monster returned.

Jo had reached Miss Morrow and was working Miss Brocas's limp arm around her neck. I hurried to catch up and managed to duck around Miss Brocas's other side, grasping her by the waist to keep her head above water. "Thank you," Miss Morrow was saying breathlessly, "thank you." Miss Brocas's eyes fluttered, but otherwise she was a dead weight between us.

"She's barely sensible," Miss Morrow gasped. "I cannot … I cannot believe it … it's so much *worse* than you described."

We all looked to where the Leviathan was breaking up a third ship by wrenching it in half. It swung one half in the air, tipping men, cannons, and goods into the open water. Their faint cries filled the air like the clamor of birds. I saw longboats being filled on the far edge of the carnage and hoped those survivors would be spared by the creature—and its controller.

"We need to get back to shore," Jo said grimly. "It's not done with Arcadia yet."

Together we pulled Miss Brocas through the water, with Miss Morrow keeping pace beside us. As we reached where the surf broke, we were nearly dragged down by Miss Brocas's weight and had to brace ourselves against the sucking water. Already, though, some Arcadians were running to help us. They were shouting and gesturing frantically, some jabbing their fingers at the bay behind us. I looked back to see the Leviathan had swung about and was lumbering towards the beach once more.

"Jo!" I cried. She didn't look back, only shoved us three forward against the water's drag. I did the same and we tumbled into the outstretched arms of the Arcadians. They helped us carry Miss Brocas into a sheltered corner beneath the headland, where Miss Morrow was already being bade sit and several wounded persons were being tended to. Up close, Miss Brocas seemed almost skeletal, her bruised, pale skin nearly bloodless, her lips a ghastly shade of blue. She made no response to the ministrations of the Arcadians as they rubbed her limbs and patted her cheeks.

Jo bent over Miss Morrow, sitting in a heap and still gasping. "We have to get inland," she said. "Can you walk at all?"

"The steps are gone," Madame Viart reported. With her rifle in her arms and her stitched cheek she looked positively ferocious. "You will have to take that other path."

"The one that cuts down, from the castle road?" a woman cried. "But that collapsed when it first attacked!"

It took a moment for my weary mind to grasp the implication: that the beach, our supposed haven, had in fact become our prison. That in all likelihood we would die here. I looked at Jo and saw a fierce resistance, her brow furrowing as she tried to work out some escape. But what could we do? We had but a few guns between us; we were exhausted and many of us injured. Our only avenue was to swim back out into the bay, where our choices were to drown or be devoured.

Madame Viart, however, was checking her weapon, a grim smile on her face. "What are you doing?" I asked.

She angled her head at the approaching Leviathan. "That one is a prima donna, she will want to finish her performance," she said tonelessly. "It would not do to deny her an audience."

"Madame," Jo said, "save your revenge for later. Right now we have to get out of its reach."

"We, we, we," Madame Viart retorted. "Speak for yourself, amateur." She made a *pfft* noise and with a toss of her head began marching back to the center of the beach.

Miss Morrow had crawled to Miss Brocas's side and was shaking her gently. "Penelope," she said. "Penelope, tell me how we stop this. You must tell me how we can stop this."

Icy water pooled around my feet, though we had moved as close to the hillside as possible. As the Leviathan drew close its tentacles stroked the water into greater and greater swells; above its head a few silent seabirds had begun to circle. Was this how soldiers felt, I wondered, when the enemy advanced? This same sort of cool stillness, the feeling of needing to scream but no sound coming?

"We have to go—" Jo began again, but I took her hand before she could finish.

"Darling," I said, "there is nowhere to go, and no time left." I smiled at her. "Besides, you did blow up all the gunpowder."

She started to speak but then stopped, her parted lips trembling, her eyes welling. "That's what happens when we separate," she whispered. "I do stupid things."

"It was a good idea at the time." I stepped close to her and laid my free hand on her cold face, still sticky with seawater. "It's all been worth it, Jo. All of it."

"I never knew love," she whispered hoarsely, "until I met you."

I kissed her then, deeply, longingly, as the water rose to our calves. The Leviathan bellowed, I waited for the end to come—

And then a voice cried, "Behold, Arcadians!"

Atop the monster stood Mrs. Masterson, her arms stretched overhead, the sword gleaming in her hand. In an unnatural synchronicity, the Leviathan raised two of its tentacles, holding them rippling in the air like the rays of some nightmarish star.

"And God asked, 'Canst thou draw out Leviathan with a hook?' Behold!" she cried. "And God asked, 'Wilt thou take him for a servant forever?' Behold!"

From our feet came a moaning sound. I tore my gaze from that terrifying display to see Miss Brocas sitting upright in the pooling water and staring at the Leviathan, feverish spots in her cheeks.

"And God said, 'None is so fierce that dare stir him up: who then is able to stand before me?" Mrs. Masterson's voice was ringing with triumph. "Behold, for I am able! Behold, for I stand before the Lord! Generations ago, we broke our covenant and our land was taken in punishment. But I will make a new covenant here and now. I will do what no mortal hand has done and I say unto God, here is a covenant in blood, now give me back our land! Give me back Arcadia!"

Jo looked at me, bewildered. "Isn't this Arcadia?" she asked.

I shook my head, as confused as she was. Again, the moaning came from below us, only this time the sounds were forming words.

"Promised me," Miss Brocas whispered. "She promised me ..."

Miss Morrow seized her hand. "What did she promise you?" she said urgently. "Think, Penelope! What is she going to do?"

She looked at Miss Morrow, and then she pointed a long, corpse-white arm at the Leviathan. "She promised me we would create a new world," she whispered. "A better world for all."

We all looked to where Mrs. Masterson was waving her arms in some complicated pattern. "I'm not sure I would call this a better world—" Jo began.

And then Mrs. Masterson brought the sword down on the Leviathan's head, driving the blade in deep.

It was as if time itself stopped. We all stared, dumbstruck, as thick, dark liquid sprayed up from the wound. The Leviathan shrieked, a howl of agony that made us clutch at our own heads. I tasted bile, though whether from its nauseating cry or sympathy for its suffering I could not say. Its young burst into a fresh cacophony of wailing—and there was a new sound too, a high-pitched sobbing that it took me a moment to realize was Miss Brocas.

The creature twisted and shuddered, trying to shake Mrs. Masterson free. A tentacle swung upwards, slapping at its own head, but Mrs. Masterson had bent over the sword, using her weight to work the blade in deeper. She was drenched in the Leviathan's purplish blood, her body almost indistinguishable from the monster's.

"Give me Arcadia!" she cried. "By this covenant of blood, *give it to me!*"

The sea began to glow.

CHAPTER XIV

A Shining Path

*I*t was as if a second sun was rising beneath the waves. The light filled the water, rendering it translucent and revealing the swirling debris of the Leviathan's attack. It grew so bright it hurt to see, yet I could not stop looking. I felt I had to look, I felt I could not turn away. The fog was thinning a little; we could see the light continued north, like a gleaming avenue running all the way to England. The water began churning again, the white foam extending far into the distance, not swells or waves, but as if many things were bubbling to the surface.

The tide rushed in, swirling around our calves, and still I could not look away.

In the distance, something shot upwards, dark and textured, and a small part of my mind noted with detached horror, *That is land. That is an outcropping of land.*

"Jo?" I whispered. "Jo, I … I think she's *raising* it." When Jo only shook her head, her lips parted in stupefied wonder, I seized her arm to make her look at me. "The map," I forced out. "The one we thought fantastical. *She is bringing it up.*"

"Bringing what up?" Miss Morrow had leapt to her feet beside us. "What is happening?"

"The map she had them hang in the tavern," Jo said, her voice awe-filled. "The one showing the Channel filled in. She's bringing up the sea floor to do just that."

Miss Morrow blinked, as if struggling to comprehend—and in truth we were all struggling to comprehend. Many around us were praying fervently, while others were frantically trying to climb to safety.

Again, the Leviathan's young cried out and again the beast moaned, its tentacles limp now, its eyes half-closed.

"How—how terrible will it be?" Miss Morrow finally asked.

At that Jo laughed strangely. I caught at her arm again, fearing for her reason, but she patted my hand. "All that water will have to go *somewhere*, Miss Morrow." She shook her head. "These islands, the south coast of England, the whole of France's coastline …"

"My God," Miss Morrow breathed. "We have to stop this."

Another hillock of land broke the surface at the edge of the bay. Water rushed onto the beach, drenching us to our thighs. I turned to help Miss Brocas stand, thinking she would drown if this kept up.

Then all sensation in my body vanished. "Jo," I said in a low voice, "we have a more immediate problem."

Jo turned and hissed in furious surprise.

Miss Brocas had risen to her feet without anyone noticing. In her hand was a knife—my knife, that I had given to Miss Morrow what felt like an age ago—and it was pressed to Miss Morrow's throat.

"Do not try to stop us," she said, her voice cracking with strain. "We are going to join her. You cannot stop us."

"We don't bloody want to," Jo retorted. "Go ahead! Just let Miss Morrow go."

"Penelope, don't do this." Though Miss Morrow's face was tight with fear, her voice was steady. "Remember what we spoke about. Love is letting people choose their fates, not forcing one upon them."

"How can you still not believe?" Miss Brocas cried, making Miss Morrow wince. "Everything is happening as foretold, everything."

"Everything is happening as she wants it to happen!" Miss Morrow replied with equal fervor. "Everything is happening because you did what she wanted, because she made you believe you would be damned for failing her!"

Behind them a rock shot up from the glowing sea, and another. Mrs. Masterson had turned her back to us and was laughing delightedly at every new appearance even as the water pushed higher and higher. The beach was fully submerged; we had to dig our feet into the wet, sucking sand to keep from being carried out with the tide. I saw Miss Brocas and Miss Morrow do the same, and then Miss Brocas took an awkward step backwards, and another, pulling Miss Morrow with her.

"Miss Brocas, please listen to Miss Morrow," I said. "You can choose to stop this."

"But why would I want to?" she wailed. "What was it all for, if not for this? I have done things …" Her voice trailed off in a moan; I felt Jo tense beside me, ready to leap, but just as swiftly Miss Brocas's eyes became focused and she tightened her grip. "I am not stopping anything," she spat out.

"We are *changing the world*. We will rule it, fairly, together."

Miss Morrow opened her mouth to protest further. Instinctively, I shook my head at her and saw her wilt in response. "Penelope," she said more gently. "Penelope, *please*. I don't want this."

They moved backwards again, in a kind of ungainly dance; we kept pace with them, now wading through knee-deep water. "Where's Viart?" Jo whispered. "She could come up from behind … if we could just signal her …"

"You will, Helena," Miss Brocas was saying. "You will. You just don't *understand* yet."

Surreptitiously I looked around. At first, I did not see Madame Viart, for I was looking for her white dress—but we were none of us white anymore, dirt and seawater had seen to that. It was the contrast with her thick black hair that I finally spotted against the tumbled hillside, which she was trying to scale.

"I think she's making for the top," I said, but just then she turned to face the sea, bracing herself against the newly-exposed dirt.

"What the hell is she doing?" Jo's voice was laced with frustration.

"I don't know." Before us, Miss Brocas had reached the first splayed tentacle and began wiggling atop it, pulling Miss Morrow up with her. "I don't think Miss Brocas will hurt her," I said, more in hope than conviction.

"The way her hand is shaking, she's liable to cut her throat by accident," Jo snapped. "We have to take that knife from her."

But things happened very quickly then:

Miss Morrow took advantage of Miss Brocas's awkward position to slip free, then turned and seized Miss Brocas's wrist, causing her to scream in fear;

Mrs. Masterson, hearing Miss Brocas's scream, moved to the edge of the Leviathan's head and peered down at them;

A large expanse of land broke above the water, causing a great swell to crest and roll towards us;

Arcadia itself shuddered, its edges further crumbling;

And from her perch, Madame Viart took aim and fired, just before debris rained down on her.

Mrs. Masterson's body leapt into the air, spraying blood, then fell atop a screaming Miss Brocas, who in turn fell against Miss Morrow. All three vanished under the water.

It was all the work of seconds. We stood there gaping at where our dear friend had once stood, at the incoming wave and the dying Leviathan, at the island crumbling around us—

And then, in silent accord, Jo and I dove under the water, just as the wave came crashing down.

How can I describe the eerie beauty of that sea? How the glow lit everything as bright as a full moon, revealing an entire realm of strange creatures and plants, a world wholly removed from humanity. The light was emanating from vast fissures, their yellow-white lines criss-crossing to form what looked like a shining path leading north and east. The fissures had cracked the sea floor into pieces that were rising up, some already above the water, others just starting to break free—and then I realized that they were no longer rising, they were in fact starting to slide back down, for without Mrs. Masterson there was no longer a covenant.

We twisted one way and another, looking desperately for Miss Morrow—and at last we saw the two of them struggling together, Miss Morrow punching and kicking while Miss Brocas held her tightly. Their twined bodies were drifting down towards one of the fissures. And if they were drawn into it? Jo and I were swimming as fast as we could, fear making us frantic as we closed the gap between us. The light painted each body in sharp relief, so I could see the naked terror on Miss Morrow's face, a strange kind of yearning on Miss Brocas's. My lungs were tightening painfully. Jo finally seized Miss Morrow's outstretched hand, kicking at Miss Brocas until she released Miss Morrow. I grabbed Jo in turn and began pulling up, up, the three of us linked together. Miss Morrow turned and offered her hand to Miss Brocas, but the latter only stared at us, her eyes wide with horror. She opened her mouth as if to speak, bubbles escaping her lips, and began falling backwards, down into the light which was dimming as the fissures narrowed beneath us.

I turned my gaze upwards. Spots danced before my eyes as we three kicked as one. Nearly there, nearly—

I broke the surface, heaving painfully, dragging Jo up beside me who pulled up Miss Morrow in turn. We each took deep breaths, gagging and coughing, yet gulping down that delicious, delicious air—

Breathe, that's my girl—

I looked at Jo, at her exhausted, bruised face, her eyes and nose reddened, snot and spit trailing down her chin. Never had she looked as beautiful, as blessedly miraculous, as at that moment.

"Bloody hell, Caroline," she whispered hoarsely.

I leaned over to kiss her, but we both paused as we realized Miss Morrow was weeping, her breath coming in hitching gasps, her eyes locked on the water and the light dimming in its depths.

"All I wanted," she gasped out, "all I wanted was to *help* her …"

At that Jo smiled sadly. "You cannot save someone who doesn't want to be saved," she said. "As you said, you have to grant them their choice."

Miss Morrow stared at her for a moment, then she flung her arms around Jo's neck and sobbed into her shoulder like a child.

I put my arms around them both, kicking to help keep us afloat, and looked around. Arcadia still stood, though her coastline was much changed. As the sea calmed and the tide began to withdraw great heaps of fallen dirt were revealed, already smoothing into a new, wider beach. The old oak tree was gone and its headland as well. I saw no sign of Madame Viart and hoped fervently that she had survived.

The great heap of the Leviathan lay unmoving, the sword jutting up from its head. The castle was eerily silent as well; indeed, it was as if a hush had fallen over the world. At the far end of the bay, I saw the drifting wreckage of Mr. Smith's ship and its fellows. Survivors had crammed into the few remaining longboats, while others were forming rafts of debris.

"We should start making for shore," I said. "We cannot last

much longer out here." Now that my fear was subsiding, I was aware of just how cold the water was. I ached everywhere and was jittery with exhaustion, which meant that Miss Morrow, having survived two prolonged bouts of swimming and struggling, must be on the verge of fainting.

But Jo only smiled at me. "Oh, I don't think we'll bother." At my surprise she angled her head. "Look south, darling."

I looked over my shoulder and found myself gaping yet again at another miraculous sight: two intact ships were approaching, some ways off but already with longboats in the water. One longboat was heading towards us, another rowing towards the wreckage of the naval ships.

I waved and hailed them. Jo began waving as well, and even Miss Morrow joined me in calling hails, though her voice was shuddering. When the boat drew close, I saw the officer was wearing an unfamiliar blue uniform but was smiling warmly at us.

"Bonjour, mesdames," he said, extending his hand. "May we escort you to safety?"

"Yes, please," Miss Morrow replied in her shuddering voice, and we all began laughing then, at the absurdity of it all, at the sheer joy of being alive.

In the longboat we were wrapped in the most delightfully warm blankets I had ever felt. I was bone-cold, cold as I had never felt before, my fingers and toes bluish from it. "It'll be 'flu all around, then," Jo remarked, and we laughed again, the same absurd laughter.

The French sailors rowed us with polite smiles and nods. Our officer gestured behind himself. "We come from the south, you from the north," he explained in deeply accented English. "We wait for the signal to act like—" He frowned, curving his forefinger and thumb and tapping them together.

"Pincer," Jo supplied, and the officer nodded.

"Yes! Pincer! Only the fog, we did not see the signal." He shook his head. "We came very late."

We were sitting in the same direction in the longboat, looking back at the French ships and the officer, our backs to Arcadia. Thus at first, we only saw that the officer's face went pale and his eyes widened, an expression we were only too familiar with now.

"Oh no," Jo muttered. With a glance at each other, all of us mirroring the other's dread, we slowly turned and looked at Arcadia.

The Leviathan was moving.

Some of its tentacles were limp, and the whole of its body seemed to be softening and greying, as if it were already decaying. Still, it used two of its tentacles to slide sideways along the beach. There it stopped for a moment, only to move again with a low, protracted moan.

Bit by bit, it slid down to the edge of the beach, with every move covering a distance as wide as a man was tall, yet for a creature of its size no more than inching along. One tentacle reached out, feeling along the sheer face of the island, probing crevices and teasing the uppermost edges of the land.

In our boat our officer barked something in a truncated

French and reached for a rifle, but Jo smacked the muzzle aside. "You cannot harm it," she said. "Even if we were closer, the shot would barely break its skin."

"It's already dying," I added. "Only what is it trying to do?"

A piece of island fell away under its probing. With another moan it wiggled the tentacle in more deeply to pull free another piece.

Faintly, so very faintly, came the keening cries of its young once more.

"It's trying to get to its children," Miss Morrow breathed. "It's trying to get into the castle."

Another chunk of trees and dirt fell into the water, and another. The creature pressed itself against the opening and pushed its tentacle inside. Fresh blood spurted up around the sword like an obscene plume. A new sound arose, a kind of high-pitched whistling, almost melodic.

And then, with a last, echoing groan, the Leviathan pulled back, bringing with it an avalanche of stone, and collapsed in a grey heap. From within the island a channel of water sluiced freely into the bay. I could not say for certain with the sun beating down, but I thought I saw several dark shapes slip through the opening.

Did I see them, or did I merely want to see them? For I suddenly wanted them to escape. I wanted it fiercely, passionately. I wanted them to live, as their parent could not; I wanted them to return to the depths of the ocean and exist as they were meant to, as they should have done, as they would have had they not become enmeshed in one family's cruel ambitions.

"My God," Jo breathed. "Did they just escape?" She looked at me with horrified eyes. "If this all starts again—"

"Darling," I interrupted, laying a hand on her arm. "Let it be."

"But ..." she trailed off, then sagged against me. "I suppose," she whispered.

"Penelope said it was called from the bottom of the sea," Miss Morrow said. Her voice was steadier, her eyes swollen but clear. "Perhaps they'll return there now?"

"As long as there are no bloody Mastersons left," Jo muttered.

"Language," I admonished.

"I've been swearing all bloody day," Jo retorted. "You cannot start scolding me now."

"We were dying then! We're not dying anymore."

"No, but we're not exactly unscathed, are we?" She swept a bruised arm over the sinking bulk of the Leviathan, the island and its shattered beach, the first of the wreckage survivors stumbling ashore. "My God," she said again, "what the hell was it all for? A few bloody rocks?"

"Now you're just needling me," I replied with a wan smile. "Perhaps Missus Masterson truly believed she could create a new land? Miss Brocas spoke of a better world ..."

"She already had a better world," Miss Morrow said. "She had a real Arcadia, one she didn't have to kill for." She laughed bitterly. "I asked Penelope that very question last night, when we were locked in the keep. Why was Missus Masterson doing this? Penelope said she had asked her long ago, when Missus Masterson first ordered her to marry Richard Loveless. And Missus Masterson had said—" She took a breath. "—she had said, 'do you ask the emperor why he conquers? Do you ask God why birth must come with blood? Because it is the order of things. As Eve lost us paradise, so her daughter will return us to paradise. That too is the order of things.'"

We fell silent at that. *Return us to paradise*—and in the name of that so-called paradise untold lives had been lost, untold destruction wreaked.

And yet without that singular, apocalyptic ambition, I might never have met Jo. I would probably be trapped in a loveless marriage, or living as an impoverished spinster dependent on my cousin's largesse. That I had found free- dom, joy, *love* all through one family's unfettered violence seemed at once both a horrifying absurdity and a terrible, awesome grace, and I understood then that here was my life's work: to not waste this gift that had been paid for in blood.

I took Jo's hand in mine; Miss Morrow leaned against me. The officer directed his men to row parallel to the beach until we were past the hump of the Leviathan, now covered with the silent seabirds who were beginning to gouge and pull at its flesh. We each of us closed our eyes, giving our fearsome antagonist a last modicum of dignity, and waited to reach dry land once more.

CHAPTER XV

Aftermaths

*T*he resourceful Arcadians had rigged a rope ladder down to the beach, and sailors were shimmying up it with admirable vigor. I, however, looked at the long, long climb and felt the last of my energy dissipate within me.

"I think I shall just stay here forever," I said to Jo despairingly. Miss Morrow had already dropped to the wet sand like a puppet with her strings cut, pulling her blanket further around herself. I sat down beside her and did the same.

"I could sleep for a year," she groaned. "And everything hurts, and this dress is not exactly modest."

For the first time I looked down at myself beneath the blanket and realized just how translucent the fabric had become. "Well," I said with a little laugh, "at least those sailors got an eyeful for their trouble?"

We began giggling then and could not stop giggling. Jo caught a passing sailor by the arm.

"I think we're going to need help," she said. He took one look at us, exhaled as if pained, and trotted off.

Jo sat down on the other side of Miss Morrow, sweeping her blanket around herself like a cape. "I'm not sure if he'll figure out a way to get us up there, or just put us back out to sea," she remarked.

"Oh," Miss Morrow said in a small voice. "I really don't want to be put back out to sea." She grimaced at the waves. "I'm not sure I can bear to sail back to England. The thought of being on water …"

She trailed off unhappily. Jo and I looked at each other over her hunched back, then we each laid an arm over her. "I don't fancy it either," Jo said.

"But if we go together, then we can be miserable together," I continued.

Miss Morrow looked from Jo to myself. "I would like that," she said, a little shyly. "Thank you both for saving me. I'm not sure I would have survived this, without you," she added with a nervous laugh.

"And we would not have succeeded without you," I said. "So thank you for aiding us, and for being brave enough to come."

She looked up at the collapsed steps. "We would all be dead now if Madame Viart hadn't shot Mrs. Masterson," she said. "Do you think—is there any chance she might have—"

"On the face of it, I would say even odds," Jo said, then grinned. "But for all her histrionics she's tough as nails, that one. I wouldn't ever bet against her."

"I dearly hope you're right," Miss Morrow said fervently.

A sailor came to us, and in a mixture of broken English and gestures he bade us come to the base of the collapsed hillside, where kind souls had rigged a sling for us and others too weary or injured to climb. We rose to our feet, steadying Miss Morrow when she staggered, and side-by-side we made our way to our makeshift deliverance.

We found the little village sadly cleaved. Gone was the tavern, as well as some of the most glorious of the oaks. The land had sheered at the barber-surgeon's, collapsing part of the little building and showing a great many emptied cabinets, for the fellow himself was treating people laid out in the square. The first intact cottage was that of the milliners, who waved us towards them with sympathetic expressions and open arms.

"You poor dears," one of the women exclaimed as we teetered forward on our bare feet, still huddled in our damp blankets. "We've got fresh tea brewing," she said, ushering us inside.

We had to step carefully, as the front room of the cottage seemed full of people: some lying on the floor wrapped in coats and blankets, others huddled together. There were bruises, weals, splinted limbs. Almost all gazed hollowly at us as we entered, with tear-filled eyes that had seen more than they could fully comprehend.

And, in one corner, was huddled a forlorn, black-haired figure dressed in dirty white cloth.

"Madame!" Miss Morrow gasped, darting across the room as if she had not been faint with exhaustion a moment before. She fell to her knees next to Madame Viart, taking her hands and speaking earnestly to her.

I started to follow but Jo laid a hand on my arm. "Let them have a moment," she murmured. "We'll get the tea and bring it over."

"Do you know Ellie?" our guide asked as she led us into the kitchen.

"She is a dear friend," I replied. "And the reason any of us are standing here now. Why is no one looking after her?"

The woman's brown face creased in sorrow. "She won't let anyone do for her," she said, lowering her voice and waving us close. "I thought at first it was shock … but then one of the fellows, he said something about how it couldn't be true, Missus Masterson must have been out of her mind, or even possessed. And Ellie gave him such a tongue lashing! After that she wouldn't even look at any of us." Her eyes gleamed with impending tears. "I know now we were duped, terribly. But for many of us, this was our last hope and our most daring dream all at once. We lost so many, and now … it's almost too much to bear …"

She dabbed at her eyes with the corner of her apron; Jo laid a hand on her shoulder. "What will happen to Arcadia now?" she asked.

"I don't know, I don't know," the woman said brokenly. "They're forming a committee, to meet with the English and French. God help us all if they turn us out."

"Surely they couldn't just—" but I was stopped by Jo's shake of the head. "There must be some legal recourse."

"It depends on whether or not it can be proved Missus Masterson owned it, for a start," Jo said. "And knowing how devious—"

"Oh, she did own it," the woman put it. "It's been in her family for generations. She had all sorts of papers about it. She would bring them to the tavern every time a ship arrived, to add our names to this large document." Suddenly she frowned. "But you should know that! We each had to sign our names."

Jo and I exchanged a look. I wanted to speak honestly about our purpose in coming to Arcadia, but in these circumstances—!

"We were undecided about staying," I said, choosing my words carefully. "Our decision to come was made in haste. We did not want to claim a residence and then change our minds, especially when there were so many others in need."

"Oh, but you must stay!" The woman stared at us, all her fear and grief momentarily forgotten. "Of course you must stay. That you got on the ship at all means you were looking for a home. Why else would you sail into the unknown on a mere promise?" She took our hands, smiling from Jo to myself and back again. "We are a *community* now. Look how we faced this day, together. Look how we are facing two of the greatest nations on earth, together. We are each other's strength."

Jo smiled back, but she disengaged her hand. "We will see, Miss, ah—"

"Missus Finchley," the woman said, angling her head. "If you see a lady darker than myself, in a yellow mob cap? That's my wife, she's the other Missus Finchley." She laughed at our surprise. "When we got married, we decided to take the name of the town we met in, rather than pick between our surnames."

I nodded, not wanting to admit that my surprise was not at their name, but that they were married at all. Until that moment I had simply never thought such a thing was possible for Jo and I, except as a temporary pretense. My weary mind could not fathom it; it seemed yet another extraordinary thing in a day of such.

Mrs. Finchley must have sensed my bewilderment, because she tugged on my hand. "And none of this talk is getting tea in you. If you could arrange some cups on that tray there, I'll pour."

I set about helping her, grateful for the activity. Soon we had a tray assembled and with profuse thanks to Mrs. Finchley carried it out to where Miss Morrow and Madame Viart were sitting. The latter was a mess of bruises and cuts, and the stitches had partially opened; still she managed a weak smile as we sat down beside her. "I told you," she murmured. "I told you I would kill her."

Miss Morrow handed her a cup of tea, then leaned in close to us. "The poor thing is nothing but cuts and bruises, and she had a nasty lump on her head. Now that you're here I am going to look for that surgeon. It's appalling that no one is taking care of her!"

Jo looked at me and I nodded. Clearly, Madame Viart had said nothing about her earlier refusals of aid. "I will come with you," Jo said, downing her tea and rising. With a downward glance she added, "and I'll see about some clothes, I cannot bear this ridiculous garb another minute."

When they left, I moved closer to Madame Viart, taking my own cup of tea. It was hot and bitter and it tasted heavenly. "Miss Morrow seems quite taken with you," I said with an encouraging smile. "It looks like you won't need my help after all."

At my words, however, the blue eyes began to well. "What does it matter?" she cried. "He will never love me now."

"Of course he will!" Still she began to weep. I tried to think of what to say, what could I say? I took her teacup from her shaking hands and put my arms around her. "If anything, he will probably desire you more."

She stared at me then, her lip curling. "You're being ridiculous."

"Am I? You were already an alluring spy. A scar will simply make you moreso." I leaned in close, lowering my voice to a whisper. "I have read many romances about female pirates, you know. They are always described as seductive, even driving men mad with desire—and bearing the scars of their adventures."

"Now you're teasing me," she sniffled, but I saw her weeping had slowed.

"Ask Jo! Why, one of our shared passions is the story of Anne Bonny and Mary Read. We even called ourselves the Reads in Medby."

At that her lips curved into something resembling her usual sly smile. "I didn't realize the English played such games," she began—and then her face crumpled again. "Sometimes … sometimes Francis and I would dress in costumes, and he would pretend—"

"Yes, yes," I said hurriedly, patting her hand. "And I am certain you will play many more, ah, games with him." I tried to catch her downcast eyes. "If he refuses you now, Madame, then he was not the man either of us thought him to be."

"I know," she said in a sodden voice. She raised her head a little, and her miserable expression contorted into something grimmer. "These people want to make excuses for her, they cannot believe a woman could trick them," she whispered. "I hate them all, I hate them! I heard a French ship has come. I am going to board it and never, ever return to this horrible place."

I was shaking my head as she spoke. "Madame—Elinor," I corrected myself. "You cannot judge them by a few distraught remarks …"

But I trailed off as I heard, amidst the muffled clamor outside, what distinctly sounded like Miss Morrow yelling. I rose to my knees to peer out of the nearest window and blurted out, "oh dear" before I could catch myself.

Francis Morrow helped another sailor off the rope ladder, then took a cane from him to lean on. Miss Morrow was running towards him, her blanket forgotten. When she flung herself into his arms, I felt my throat tighten. Behind Miss Morrow came Jo, wiggling and tugging at the dress I knew she hated. She shook the hand Mr. Morrow extended to her. I saw my love wipe roughly at the back of her eyes, and my own welled in grateful sympathy that she had been able to keep her promise, and deliver Mr. Morrow's sister safely back to him.

But what of my own charge? I looked down at the wan, bruised woman huddled next to me, and then I knew what I must do. I crouched down before her. "Elinor," I said, taking her hands. "I must be honest with you. Francis Morrow has just arrived—" At her gasp of fright I held her hands tightly, so she could not pull away— "and I think we should go meet him. I will be with you," I added when she shook her head in protest. "I will be right there with you. And if he reacts poorly, then you will come away with Jo and I. We won't leave you alone. I promise."

She stared at me, those bright blue eyes spilling endlessly. As lovely as a porcelain shepherdess, only with a few cracks and scuffs now. Somehow it made her seem more beautiful, not an idealized object but a flesh-and-blood person.

"Come," I said encouragingly, helping her to her feet. I tucked her arm under mine, careful not to put pressure on the livid bruises. Oh, how she was trembling! Faced with a nightmarish monster she had coolly taken aim and fired, but possible rejection from the man she loved and she was terrified. If Mr. Morrow refused her—if he so much as *flinched* upon seeing her—

We stepped out into the late afternoon sunlight. As the light struck her face she cried out softly and tried to turn back, only I held her firm. How could I distract her … and then I remembered something that had been puzzling me.

"You told me, back in the cells," I said, "that Monsieur Viart was a brute. Why, then, do you use his name?"

She gaped at me, her own fears momentarily forgotten. "But of course I kept his name. I poisoned him," she said, as if it such a thing was an obvious deduction. "It was my rightful trophy …" She trailed off then, her hand drifting to her face.

"Trophies can come in many forms, Madame," I suggested. "Shall we greet Mister Morrow?"

She took a deep, shuddering breath, raised her chin, and fell into step beside me. Slowly we began to traverse the square. Mr. Morrow was arguing with his sister; it seemed that now that he was assured of her health and safety, he was furiously venting all his worries upon her, and she was replying in kind. I caught Jo's gaze and she smiled at me, then angled her head at them and rolled her eyes.

We were halfway across the square when we heard it: the slow, steady beat of a pair of hands clapping. Philip had risen to his feet in the middle of a group of seated Arcadians and was applauding us. When our eyes met, he bowed to Madame Viart, then continued his applause. Swiftly others rose to their feet, applauding and calling, "Thank you, Ellie!" and "God bless you, Madame!" My charge gave a little sob, then made a stiff, yet elegant curtsey that earned her more applause—

—and then Mr. Morrow was standing before us.

He was thinner than I remembered, and he held himself oddly—but he was not yet fully healed himself. Beneath his wig, I glimpsed the first touches of grey at his temples, and wondered what would be writ on my own face now.

"Miss Daniels," he said, but his eyes were fixed upon Madame Viart's face. I saw no horror or pity in his own, only sympathy and—

And love.

"Mister Morrow," I said, gently undoing my arm from my companion's. "Perhaps you can help Madame find a doctor?"

But he did not seem to hear me. He cupped Madame Viart's face tenderly, careful not to touch the stitches. "I'm so sorry, Ellie," he said huskily. "I am so, so sorry. I should have been here, I should never have told you to start without me—I didn't *think*—"

She pressed a trembling hand over his mouth. He kissed her fingertips, then bowed his head to hers. I turned away from them only to find Jo smiling at me, a smile that warmed me through.

"I have an idea," she purred, drawing me away from the others.

"Oh?" I knew my cheeks were reddening. People glanced at us, then politely looked away.

"Smith just landed, the French are already muttering about jurisdictions and maritime law, and I have no patience for any of it," she said, then held up an armful of fabric. "On the other hand, I have some spare clothes of our friend Philip's, only I haven't found anyplace private to change in." Her free hand snaked around my waist. "What say we find a quiet corner and take these damn dresses off?"

"Jo Chase," I declared breathlessly, "you are brilliant."

"I have learned from the best." She kissed my cheek, then nipped at my earlobe, making me gasp. "Let's go be alone, together."

CHAPTER XVI

Promises Deserved

We did indeed find a secluded hollow to change in, and then, at last, we got some much-needed rest—after some equally needed affection. Each touch felt an affirmation: *we are alive, we survived*. When we finally awoke, the setting sun had tinted the whole of the bay a deep orange and cast the anchored French ships in sharp relief. Another English ship had arrived and anchored at the northern end of the bay, and we could just glimpse the village square bright with lamps and torches.

Beyond it all, the fog wall remained: softer, thinner in spots, more drifting cloud than opaque barrier; still it ringed the island as far as we could see. Could it truly be a natural phenomenon? Whatever its cause, it was but little affected by Mrs. Masterson's passing.

"Leave them to it," Jo said with a yawn. She rose and stretched, the sleeves of Philip's too-large shirt falling away from her forearms. With a glance around us, she picked up a stone larger than her fist.

"What are you doing?" I asked, my stomach punctuating the question with a growl.

She grinned. "Philip gave me directions to his cottage.

Maybe we can sneak around there and beg some supper off him?" She knotted her dress around the stone, then flung the bundle high into the sky. We watched it arc and then drop into the water.

"It wasn't that bad of a dress," I said lightly. "With a great deal of washing, we could have used it for rags."

Her expression, however, was serious as she dropped back down beside me. "I cannot wear them anymore, Caro." She smiled wanly at me. "When they put it on me last night it felt *awful*. I wanted to claw it off, modesty be damned, and I promised myself if we survived all this, then no more. Suits feel right. 'Jo' feels right. Dresses, Joanna, Miss Chase—those all feel wrong now." She bit her lip. "I know I'm not making sense—"

"You're making perfect sense." I took her hand. "Darling, you can wear whatever you please, and I will call you whatever you wish. All that matters to me is that you're happy."

Her expression softened then. She kissed me, her hand fishing under the smock Philip had kindly lent for my own use—

A voice cleared behind us and we quickly broke apart.

"Our apologies for interrupting, only we thought you would be hungry," Miss Morrow said, holding up a basket.

"And that you had the right idea, getting away from that mess," Mr. Morrow added, angling his head behind him.

"Where is Madame Viart?" I demanded.

"She wanted off the island, so I arranged a private cabin for her," he said, pointing to the English ship. "The doctor on board cleaned that cut and stitched it properly. We'll be staying there tonight, if you want to come with us."

"*You* will be staying there," Miss Morrow said, kneeling

beside us and unpacking the basket. The smell of bread had me reaching before I remembered my manners.

"Helena, we have been over this—"

"*I* am spending the night here," she said firmly. "The committee is meeting after supper to discuss Arcadia's future. I want to be there."

He fell silent, his jaw working. Jo asked, "Meeting with representatives of France and England, I'm guessing?"

She handed us each part of a loaf, then produced a pot of butter. I was already ripping off a chunk and eating it. Never in my life had a simple loaf tasted as heavenly. "Oh my, yes, though both parties will be furious. Did you hear about Missus Masterson's will? Apparently, she left a very detailed one, with explicit instructions for the future of the 'country of Arcadia.' She was probably thinking of a much larger Arcadia, of course. But it's still perfectly legal: she owned this island outright. It was never annexed even when the surrounding islands were being claimed—"

"The fog," Jo murmured.

"—which means as things stand, if either power tries to contest matters it could be tied up in the courts for years." She grinned at us. "Your fellow Smith and his French counterpart are both having kittens! I wouldn't miss tonight for anything."

"Except it has nothing to do with you," Mr. Morrow snapped.

"Frannie, *sit down*," she replied, clearly exasperated. At her tone he dropped beside her with a grimace. "He's upset," she explained, "because I told him that when we get back to London, I am doing three things: hugging my mama very tight, marrying Gerald, and moving us and our parents here."

"Moving here?" I exclaimed, while Jo said, "but why?"

"Why is everyone so surprised? This place, it has so much *possibility*, don't you see?" Her eyes gleamed in the twilight. "We have a chance to really *build* something here. They don't even have a grocer yet, they were ecstatic when I brought up the possibility. We could start fresh in a place where we would be appreciated—appreciated and *safe*." She took a breath, then shook herself. "And I am a terrible hostess. There is also potted meat, and salad …"

She brought out two more little clay bowls and a fistful of cutlery. I smeared my bread liberally with potted meat and oh! It was as if my very body were being returned to me, mouthful by mouthful; my body and my reason, as I was finally able to ponder Miss Morrow's plan, and Mrs. Finchley's earlier speech. The things they spoke of—safety, appreciation, community—made something resonate deep within me. Community—a *home* …

Jo swallowed an enormous mouthful of bread, then remarked, "It's not the worst idea, Morrow."

There was a pained sigh from his shadowed form, his dark brown face unreadable in the deepening twilight. "No, it's not," he said unwillingly.

"It's not like it will make much difference to you," Miss Morrow tossed over her shoulder. "You can as easily visit us here as in London. In fact, we may be a little closer to France."

"It's just … it's just so *small*," he said, looking around.

"It's not small, it's lovely! Think of the hours our poor

parents work now. Gerald could probably manage entirely without them—"

Mr. Morrow snorted.

"—which of course they won't let happen, but it means they won't have to *worry*, Frannie." She hesitated, then said in a smaller voice, "and I could paint what I want, not just draw wallpaper for noblemen."

I smiled at that. I saw, too, Mr. Morrow's hand snake out and squeeze his sister's. "I think Miss Brocas would have been happy for you," I said.

Miss Morrow started to speak but instead nodded, visibly overcome with emotion.

"What about you two, then?" Mr. Morrow asked. "More work for Smith?"

"Absolutely not," I said, while Jo said, "We had already decided we're out with this one."

"Then you could move here too!" Miss Morrow exclaimed. "The committee said they will give a plot to any of us as a token of their gratitude. There are even a couple of houses left! They need work, but the walls are quite sound."

Again, I felt that twinge of resonance inside. A home … oh, it set off a cascade of mingled emotions, the sensation of many doors both closing and opening. I looked at Jo, who mouthed *your decision* and I mouthed *decide together* and she shrugged. "It makes no odds to me, Caro," she said. "Home is where you are."

I started to speak, then broke off as I heard it. "Is that a bird?"

We all listened intently, trying to separate the faint sounds from the surf below. At last Mr. Morrow pointed above us.

"There. Flying to their nests for the night."

The tiny black shapes sailed over our heads, calling to each other; the sound tugged at my heart. A kind of healing, to hear birds once more. I was suddenly reminded of walking through our garden at twilight many years ago, longing to fly myself, longing for a reason to sing. I looked at the land around us: it was small, but I had been raised in a small world. Would Jo be as content, however? A community, one we could help build. The idea eased an ache in my heart, even as I remembered how, too, sometimes communities could confine, even smother you.

"Perhaps someday," I finally said, then looked at Jo. "However, I was once at a dinner party with this enigmatic yet alluring young man, who spoke at length about his travels in Italy."

It was too dark to make out her expression, but I felt certain that Jo was blushing. "I have it on good account," she said, "that the young man in question was bragging, to try to turn the head of his beautiful hostess."

"Always a good tactic, Chase," Mr. Morrow put in, yelping when Miss Morrow smacked his arm.

"It was always my intent that someday, if fate and fortune allowed, I would remind the young man that the proof of the pudding is in the eating, and he should show me these sights that so enthralled him." I paused, gazing at Jo. "If indeed he was ever in Italy at all."

At that she laughed, low and throaty; it warmed something deep inside me. "Are you calling me a liar, Caroline Daniels? Because I warn you, such a challenge will not go unanswered."

"Or maybe, Jo Chase, I just want you to take me to Italy."

"Oh, I will take you, darling—"

"May I remind you both that my sister is present," Mr. Morrow said, ducking another swipe from Miss Morrow. "And I think we should head back soon, before we lose sight of the path completely."

We packed up the remains of the food. As Jo helped me up, she said, "I did have one question, Morrow. How was it that you were on that ship? You couldn't have gotten our letters so soon."

"I never got your letters at all," he replied, taking the basket from Miss Morrow and crooking his arm at her.

"Then how did you know to come?"

His sister slipped her arm through his and we struck out for the village. "I knew because this one has trouble keeping her stories straight," he replied lightly. "She told our parents she was going to Twickenham to spend the weekend sketching with Miss Roche and her family ... but she forgot that she had once told me, over too many sherries, that she can barely stand Miss Roche, who laughs like a horse and thinks herself bold for repeating the servants' dirty jokes, am I remembering aright?" Miss Morrow merely sniffed, which made him laugh. "And then I found a pamphlet about Arcadia in her room, and I was on the next coach south."

Miss Morrow smacked his arm yet again. "You never said you went through my things!"

"I didn't, Hel. You dropped the pamphlet on the floor. Which was another worrisome sign: you're usually much cleverer than that."

Mollified, Miss Morrow pressed close to him. I smiled to see it, and how her brother patted her arm in turn. "So where will you go now, Mister Morrow?" I asked.

"Back to Paris with Elinor."

"Does she want to go back?"

"You mean her injury? Oh, she is still upset about it—as am I, it's a good thing she shot that woman, otherwise—" He paused, taking a breath. "We made a bargain: if she will try going back for a season, she can tell whatever story she likes about the scar and I'll vouch for her." He grinned at us over his shoulder. "Believe me, by spring every fashionable woman in Paris will be painting a scar on her cheek and telling her own tall tales."

"You never vouched for any of my stories," Miss Morrow said haughtily.

"Because you always kept the best sweets for yourself," he retorted. "You never learned to pay your henchmen."

Jo slowed our pace, letting the distance grow between ourselves and their gentle bickering until we were out of earshot. "You like it here, don't you?" she murmured.

"It reminds me of home," I murmured back. "Damaged bays and all. My father would have loved all of this: planning a community, debating wills and treaties …" I looked at her, straining to make out her face in the darkness. "Could you live here?"

"I could certainly try." She hesitated. "Besides Missus Finchley, I saw at least two other couples like us and everyone behaved normally towards them. We could do far worse. But it's also a big world, Caroline Daniels."

I looped her arm around my shoulders. "With plenty of

adventures to be had. But tell me, Jo Chase, what are adventures without someplace to come home to?"

"Are you suggesting we hedge our bets?"

"You know, I think I am."

"A country girl with a gambler's heart," she purred. "So, what: take a cottage here, then off to Italy?"

"I was thinking more just a plot of land for now." I snuggled close. "Are we planning our future?"

For a moment she was silent, then she said, wonderingly, "You know, I don't remember the last time I thought of a future. First there was keeping my family together, then the whole fiction of Jonathan Chase, and then everything became about the Mastersons."

"While I was trying not to think of the future at all, since mine was to be either an unhappy marriage or an unhappy spinsterhood." I was suddenly on the verge of tears. "Jo?"

She stopped us, turning to me. "Darling, what is it?"

"We—we deserve this, don't we?" I could barely form the words. I felt, oh, how could I even describe what I felt? I could not parse my fears from my sorrows from a growing, glorious hope. "After everything that's happened … so many dead, so much violence …"

She kissed me then, fiercely. When at last we broke apart, she said, "We deserve it, Caroline. We deserve *all* of it. We have been through hell and we survived it together. It is our future and we deserve every moment of it. Caroline, marry me."

The words came out so quickly I nearly missed them. "What?" I blurted out.

"Marry me." She dropped to her knees on the dirt path and

took my hands. The rising moonlight showed me all I needed to see in her face, so lovely and full of hope and yearning that I began to weep. "Here, Italy, wherever you like. Marry me, darling. Because I love you. Because I will always love you. Because *we deserve it*."

And oh, dear reader, if you have stayed with us through all of this? Know that in this moment of pure joy, with our hard-fought battles behind us and the promise of tenderer days ahead, facing this precious future that I knew we would both die to protect—

Know that I was in that moment and forevermore still my father's child, for what came unbidden to my lips was the Shakespeare he so loved:

I would not wish
Any companion in the world but you.

ACKNOWLEDGMENTS

I began these stories in the wake of the 2016 election here in the U.S. It was a dark, terrifying time, and I desperately needed to put some light in the world; I desperately needed a story where the women won. I told myself I was writing a romance—or as much of a romance as this grim, weird writer can manage—but what I came to realize is that romance, for me, is less about will-they-won't-they and more about relationships: how they deepen over time, weathering trials and developing their own language ... and that wasn't something I could fully explore in just one novella. Thus one book became two, and two became four, until at last I felt I could lower the curtain and give Caroline and Jo a well-deserved rest.

It meant everything to me that so many who helped me through *Harkworth Hall* have stayed with me through all four books. Thus Kat Howard once again provided her editorial feedback; Charlotte Ashley copyedited with her usual gentle hand and by now well-worn admonishments; and Najla and Nada Qamber designed cover and interior respectively. Manu Velasco returned to help me with issues of representation; every time I work with them I feel myself becoming a better writer. And a special thanks is due to Shane McMurray at the Caird Library in Greenwich, who pointed me towards resources that swiftly answered my questions about Dorset and the Channel Islands. Someday, hopefully, I'll be able to do justice to all his suggestions in another tale.

And here, dear readers, is where I must confess: I am terrible at goodbyes. So instead I will say: Caroline and Jo, be happy, be light, and perhaps our paths will cross again—

California
February 2022

ABOUT THE AUTHOR

L.S. Johnson lives in California with a spouse, a cat, and numerous goldfish. She is the author of the Chase & Daniels quartet of gothic novellas and over 40 short stories, many of which can be found in her collections *Vacui Magia* and *Rare Birds*. Her vampire serial, Prima Materia, is happening now at primamateria.online. You can sign up for her newsletter and learn about her upcoming appearances at traversingz.com.

Made in the USA
Columbia, SC
24 January 2024

30164587R00124